The
Lumberjerk

CHRIS DOTSON

TO JOHN KENNEDY TOOLE

1

He was dead when they found him.

Well, he wasn't really dead. They just thought he looked that way. So to say that they found him *dead* wouldn't be a fair statement.

He was *alive* when they found him. And why wouldn't he be? He'd asked them to meet him at Pizza Munch. Who dies at *Pizza Munch*? Nobody. And certainly not him.

"I don't appreciate that remark," said Steve, when they told him he looked dead. "I just came from the gym. I'm actually feeling pretty good."

He went on to tell the two men that he always went to Pizza Munch after the gym. He said it was because his metabolism was always high after working out so he could eat an entire large supreme pizza and only gain a fraction of the weight he normally would have gained if he hadn't worked out.

"So why did you call us here?" said the first man.

"Well," said Steve as he took a sip from his beverage, "here's the thing: someone urinates in the pool at my gym and I think I know who it is."

"Huh?" said the first man.

"Some sick fuck. Some *Pool Pisser.* He's going around pissing in the pool and I can smell it."

"What are you talking about?" said the second man. "First of all, if you're talking about a pool at your gym, it's probably huge. Even if someone *does* urinate in the pool, how can you smell it unless you're right next to him when he does it? And what about chlorine? Doesn't that eat urine?"

"Fair questions. But let's just say I'm on to this guy. Or let's at least just say I've got it narrowed down to roughly fifteen people."

The server brought the pizza that Steve had ordered.

Steve grabbed the spatula and offered the men slices.

They declined.

"So you called us down here to tell us some guy is pissing in the pool at your gym?" said the first man.

"I want you to kill him," said Steve. "I want to teach this guy a lesson."

He chewed his pizza in silence as the men contemplated Steve's proposal.

"You sure you guys don't want a slice? What about a lemonade? It's free refills!"

"Regardless of what you might think about us," said the second man, "we're not in the business of killing people because they go wee-wee in a public pool."

"Fifty-four thousand dollars," said Steve. "Fifty-four thousand. That's my life savings. And it can be yours. All you have to do is take this guy out. I'll give you half now and half after the job is done."

Steve took another bite of his pizza and reconsidered. Maybe half now was too much. "No, wait. Half is twenty-seven thousand. That's kind of a lot of money. I'm not giving you all that money right now. I'll give you five thousand. No, six thousand right now and then I'll give you the remaining forty-eight thousand when it's done."

The two men looked at each other, considering the offer. Then the server came back to the table and asked if she could bring anyone anything else.

"Two lemonades," the men said in unison.

2

They walked to the Pizza Munch parking lot. Steve opened his car door, reached under the passenger seat, and pulled out a large manila envelope overflowing with hundred-dollar bills.

"Okay, six thousand dollars." Steve began counting out the money on the trunk of the car. "One hundred, two hundred, three hundred, four hundred…"

The two men did not like this.

"What the hell are you doing?" said the first man.

"What does it look like I'm doing? I'm giving you your money."

"He means, why are you doing it like *this*? Counting it in the open?" said the second man.

"I'm sorry," said Steve, raising the volume of his voice significantly. "Maybe it's because I don't give a fuck! Maybe it's because I don't have any tolerance for people who piss in a pool that I pay good money to use!"

"You're causing a scene," said the first man. "And we're going to need at least sixty-four hundred up front because of it."

"Fine," said Steve. He finished counting out the money and handed it to them just as a mother walked by with her son, who was probably five years old.

Steve crouched down in front of the boy.

"Little boy," said Steve, "let me give you some advice. When you grow up, never, ever piss in a public pool. Because there are people in this world who don't take very kindly to that kind of behavior."

The boy nodded. Steve looked at the mother and smirked.

"You single?"

The mother grabbed the boy's hand and the two of them hurried off.

"She was wearing a wedding ring," said the second man.

"Hey, rings come off!" said Steve.

3

Steve's wife Kelly prepared a dinner for him that evening. She was trying to get Steve to eat more carrots. She had read somewhere that carrots prevented memory loss. Several people on Steve's side of the family had developed Alzheimer's disease over the years, including the two Scotties that were Steve's childhood dogs.

Kelly was not going to let Steve go down that same road without putting up a fight.

So she chopped up a one-pound bag of carrots and mixed them with a bag of salad greens. She knew Steve would appreciate a nice meal after a long day.

When Steve arrived home, he was in a good mood. Kelly had not seen him like this in some time. She wondered if perhaps someone had given him a foot massage at work. She'd heard that more and more companies were bringing masseuses into their offices to massage their employees while they worked at their computers.

"Well, you certainly have a spring in your step," said Kelly as Steve entered the kitchen.

"I had a great day, honey. Just a wonderful day."

"You must be hungry! Sit down. I made you a carrot salad."

Steve gritted his teeth. "For the love of God, Kelly. What day is it?"

Kelly thought for a moment. "I believe it's Wednesday."

"Yes, Kelly. It's *Wednesday*. And what happens on Wednesdays?"

It was all coming back to her now. "You go to the gym on Wednesdays."

"That's right," said Steve. "I go to the gym. And what happens after I go to the gym?"

"You go to Pizza Munch."

"That's right. I go to Pizza Munch. And guess what? Since today is Wednesday, I went to the gym and then I went to Pizza Munch and now I'm full. So I couldn't possibly eat a carrot salad."

"Oh, Steve, but what about the Alzheimer's?"

"What *about* the Alzheimer's? You're the one who forgot what day it is. Maybe *you* should have some carrots. Go on, eat the whole fucking bag!"

Steve walked upstairs. Kelly stared at the bowl of uneaten salad. She decided she would put it in a large plastic container. Steve could take it to work with him tomorrow. Maybe if he could have his "Pizza Munch Wednesdays," she could start a new tradition for him called "Carrot Salad Thursdays." She decided she would approach Steve with this idea first thing in the morning.

4

Although Kelly had made up her mind earlier in the evening that she wouldn't talk to Steve about "Carrot Salad Thursdays" until the following morning, she now found herself lying in bed next to him and she knew in her heart that she wouldn't be able to sleep until the topic had been broached. But it wasn't really carrots that were bothering her—it was Pizza Munch.

"Steve," she said, "why can't I meet you at Pizza Munch one of these Wednesdays? Why do you always have to go alone?"

Steve sighed. "Because that's what Pizza Munch is for, Kelly. It's a place to be alone. It's a place for contemplation. Pizza Munch is where I go to be with my thoughts."

"Well, I'd like to be a part of your thoughts, too, Steve. I mean, I used to be. You used to share things with me, but you don't share with me anymore. I don't think it's fair."

"Aw, honey. I'm in bed. I'm trying to relax. I've got a big day tomorrow and now you decide you're gonna go ahead and completely blindside me with this Pizza Munch thing? What is it? Is it because I didn't eat the carrots? I'll eat some fucking carrots for breakfast, okay? You can put 'em in the goddamn blender and I'll have a fucking carrot smoothie. Okay?"

Steve rolled over, determined to go to sleep.

Kelly then did something she had never done before. She took the magazine she was reading, rolled it up, and began to hit Steve with it as hard as she could.

"Kelly! What the hell has gotten into you?" Steve yelled as Kelly thrashed away.

Kelly got in several more solid whacks before running into the bathroom and locking the door behind her.

Steve went to the bathroom door and jiggled the handle. "Kelly! Kelly! Open up!"

Kelly didn't open up.

"Fine, you want to sleep in the bathroom? Sleep in the bathroom!"

Steve returned to bed, but he wasn't able to fall asleep right away. So he took the magazine that had just been used as a weapon against him, flattened it out, and read an article titled *How to Get Hot Legs in 30 Days*.

5

Steve had a fitful sleep. He dreamed he was on a cruise ship and he was in charge of running a bingo game. It was his job to spin the bingo cage and announce the ball. But whenever a ball rolled out of the cage, it wasn't a bingo ball. It was a gumball and Steve would eat it. The players started to become very irritated. Then Steve turned into a baleen whale and found himself craving ketchup.

Steve hated dreams.

"I had the whale dream again," he said to Kelly as he opened his eyes and rolled over in bed. Kelly wasn't there. Steve then remembered she'd locked herself in the bathroom the previous night. He walked back to the bathroom, attempted to turn the knob, and once again found the door locked.

"Kelly! Let me the fuck in right now," Steve hollered.

There was no response. He pounded on the door. Still nothing. "Kelly, this is the last thing I need today! I've got a big day ahead of me. A *big* day. And you go and pull this stunt? Get out of there!"

Kelly did not respond.

"Fine," yelled Steve. "I'll use the bathroom in the hallway!"

Steve did not like using the bathroom in the hallway. For one thing, none of his toiletries were in there. In the shower, there were no bars of soap—only body wash. Steve had never cared for body wash. He didn't like how it lathered and he didn't like how it smelled. Kelly had once suggested he use a loofah to increase the lather, but Steve would hear nothing of it. "Those things look like cow's vaginas," Steve yelled. That had ended that conversation.

But now Steve found himself squeezing grapefruit custard body wash into his hand. He hated its feminine smell, hated that it didn't lather the way he wished it would, and most of all he hated that he couldn't use his own shower in his own house. He had to use the guest shower, all because his wife decided last night that they should start "sharing" again.

Maybe he should have eaten a few carrots last night, he thought to himself. Would it have killed him? Still, he'd never seen Kelly have an outburst like that. She'd never hit him with anything before. He'd never seen her lose her temper before. Something was wrong.

"Cancer," he said out loud as he toweled himself off. "She must have cancer." What else could account for such erratic behavior? All the warning signs were there: she was pushing fifty years of age, she didn't exercise, and she was *pushing fifty years of age*!

Steve realized he should be glad *he* didn't have cancer. Hell, every middle-aged person seemed to be getting it these days for seemingly no reason at all. It had taken some time, but Steve finally figured out what was wrong with his wife. He walked back to the master bathroom to share the news with her.

6

"Kelly," said Steve through the bathroom door, "I'm sorry I yelled at you earlier, but I need you to do something for me. I need you to knock one time if you're okay in there."

Steve wasn't sure what he'd do if Kelly didn't knock. Maybe he'd kick the door in. He could have already kicked it in if he'd really wanted to, but he didn't see any reason to go around kicking in good doors and having to go out and buy new ones just because his wife was having issues. And if he were to find out that she did indeed have cancer, he knew he would feel particularly rotten for having been so insensitive to her condition by kicking in a door.

Steve realized if this cancer was a reality, he'd have to reconsider his plan to eliminate the Pool Pisser because they would need every penny they had to pay Kelly's medical bills. Steve certainly wasn't a doctor, but he did know one thing: cancer wasn't cheap.

Fortunately for Steve, the knock came. She was still kicking in there.

"That's great, honey. That's great. Now, knock twice if you have cancer."

There was no knock. Perhaps she'd misunderstood his instructions.

"Kelly, if you have cancer, I need you to knock twice on the

15

door. Can you do that for me?"

Again, there was only silence.

Steve threw his hands up. "Well, I'm at a loss, Kelly. I'm at a fucking loss. You're telling me that you don't have cancer? Then what was that show you put on last night? And why is this show still going on *today*?"

Steve gave the door a healthy kick before giving up. He decided to get dressed and go to work. He figured the sooner he left the house, the sooner Kelly would come out. He wouldn't be able to shave today; his razor was behind that door. But that was fine. What really irritated him was that he wouldn't be able to splash cologne on his face.

He decided when he got home that evening he'd take a bottle of cologne and put it in his nightstand just in case a situation like this presented itself again. Steve had no idea if this outburst was a sign of things to come, and he wanted to be prepared for anything. He had no intention of being separated from his cologne ever again.

7

Steve's father never permitted Steve to own a baseball glove. This made for some very painful games of catch between father and son. Steve's father never gave an explanation as to what he had against baseball gloves, other than he'd "never trusted them."

Despite his aversion to baseball gloves, Steve's father loved the game and would take Steve to several minor league baseball games a year. Steve was not allowed to eat any concessions at the game. "Stadium food is overpriced," his father would tell him, "and it's not made with love." It was very important to Steve's father that Steve only eat food that was made with love. And unfortunately for Steve, his father felt that food made with love could not be found outside the home. This was a major reason why Steve never ate at a diner until the age of eighteen.

Steve's father also encouraged Steve to play little league baseball. Steve was primarily used as a designated hitter. His coaches were very hesitant about playing Steve in the field, fearing he'd injure his gloveless hand.

One year, Steve's team was coached by a man named Dale. Dale made the mistake of lending Steve a glove and then put him in as the second baseman. Steve's father, running late from work, arrived at the game in the third inning to find Steve wearing a baseball glove and immediately charged the field, ripped the glove from his son's hand, held the glove aloft, and demanded that the person who gave his son the glove step forward.

Dale, finding the whole display rather humorous, walked onto the field and told Steve's father that he was the one who supplied Steve with the mitt. Steve's father proceeded to spit in Dale's face, which probably wasn't the best idea considering Dale was almost a foot taller than him.

Dale, despite being a man of humor, had his limits, and to him, a spit in the face was worthy of a kick to the testicles, and that's exactly what Steve's father received.

From that day forward, Steve's father became known as "The Spitter," and Steve became known as "The Son of the Spitter." Although the nickname was unflattering, Steve found it preferable to being known as "The Son of the Guy Who Got Kicked in the Nuts."

So none of Steve's coaches ever again attempted to lend Steve a glove. They instead had him bat exclusively and never permitted him to play in the field.

Steve's father was a pharmacist.

8

"Being a pharmacist is not easy," Steve's father could often be heard saying at the dinner table. "It requires ingenuity, courage, and a tremendous amount of self-respect."

Why exactly being a pharmacist required those traits, Steve never knew. Nor did he care to find out. When Steve was fourteen years old, he quit playing baseball entirely. Not that any of his teammates or coaches missed him. By that point, Steve had proven himself a rather worthless hitter. Add in the fact that he couldn't be used in the field, and Steve found himself "riding the pine" as his father called it.

After the spitting incident and subsequent kick to the balls, Steve's father stopped attending Steve's games. He would instead stay home and paint tiny wooden boats. Steve's father never painted tiny wooden boats prior to being kicked in the nuts by Dale, but after that day, tiny wooden boats suddenly appeared all over the house and Steve's father would tell Steve that as much as he supported Steve and wanted to cheer him on during his games, these tiny wooden boats were not going to paint themselves. Surely Steve could understand.

But Steve did not understand. Steve felt that playing baseball was difficult enough even if one had a supportive father who permitted him to wear a baseball glove. Lacking both a glove and a supportive father, Steve began to wonder what the point of playing the game was. Disillusionment set in. And once a fourteen-year-old boy becomes disillusioned, there's no going back.

One day Steve came home from another baseball game—another game where his team got slaughtered, and another game where Steve was not called upon to bat.

"How did it go today?" his father asked, barely looking up from painting one of his boats.

"Okay," said Steve.

"Did they let you hit or did you ride the pine?"

"Rode the pine."

"Nothing wrong with riding the pine, Steve. Plenty of pine riders have gone on to do great things."

"I quit today."

"You quit? What do you mean you quit?"

"I told the coach I wasn't going to be on the team anymore."

"So you're going to walk away from it, just like that?"

Steve shrugged.

Steve's father put down his boat.

"Listen, Steve. I know you ride the pine. But sometimes that's what baseball is about. It's about *not* playing. It's about not feeling like you're a part of the team. It's about not enjoying the game at all. And sometimes, yes, it's about being a pine rider. Do you follow me?"

Steve had absolutely no interest in following his father.

"And I guess what you're going to tell me next is that baseball isn't about wearing a baseball glove, either," said Steve.

Steve's father slammed his hand on the table as hard as he could. Tiny wooden boats went flying everywhere. Several drops of paint splattered on his father's white dress shirt. (Damnit, he had to remember to wear a smock when he was working with his boats.)

"You are absolutely correct, young man! That is *exactly* what I was about to say!" Steve's father looked down at his hand that he'd driven so violently into the table. It hurt quite a bit. But he wasn't about to rub it or let Steve know how much it pained him. Perhaps if he just tried reasoning with the boy.

"Look, Steve. I've done a lot of things I'm not proud of. It's just this constant pressure that I'm under as a pharmacist. It's..."

"Mom would understand," said Steve.

"You're wrong. Your mother wouldn't understand. Your mother was a wonderful woman, but she would not understand why her son would want to be known as a quitter."

"Well, I'd rather be known as a quitter than be known as a *spitter*!" Steve yelled as he stormed upstairs to his bedroom.

"Steven! Steven!" Steve's father momentarily considered chasing after him, but then decided this would be the perfect opportunity to ice his sore hand without the boy seeing.

Being a pharmacist is not easy.

9

There was a thirty-foot oak outside Steve's bedroom window. The oak was not originally there when his mother and father moved into the house. In fact, it wasn't there at all until after his mother died.

Steve knew very little about his mother, other than she had died when Steve was either two or three years of age. Whenever he asked his father about his mother, the only thing he would tell him was that she was a "wonderful woman."

But Steve did know quite a bit about the thirty-foot oak outside his bedroom window. The tree had belonged to his mother's parents. Or at least, it was on their property. His mother had grown up with the tree and loved to play in it as a child. Steve's father and mother were married beneath it.

The reason the tree now resided in the yard outside Steve's bedroom was that Steve's father had the tree uprooted after Steve's mother died, and then had it transported four hundred miles and replanted in their backyard.

Steve's father was quite grief-stricken after losing his wife and he decided he needed something close to him that would keep her memory alive. Most widowers in his position could look at old family photos to conjure up happy memories of their deceased spouse, but Steve's mother never permitted anyone to take her picture, not even at her wedding.

In lieu of owning any photos of his late wife whatsoever, Steve's father decided that having possession of the tree was the next best thing. He came to an arrangement with the current owner of the house (his wife's parents had died several years before she did, and hadn't been the owners of that house for years) and that's how Steve's mother's family's oak tree ended up in Steve's backyard.

Steve was staring at the tree now, wishing he had a different father, wishing he knew more about his mother, and wishing he had a picture of her. But all he had was this tree. Steve had considered talking to the tree over the years and addressing it as if it were his mother.

Steve knew it was rather pointless to attempt to converse with a thirty-foot oak, but seeing as how tonight he was experiencing disillusionment for the first time in his young life, he decided this would be the perfect opportunity to dialogue with it.

"Tree," said Steve, "I mean… mom…"

Steve sighed. Even though tonight had been one of the worst nights of his life, he still couldn't bring himself to talk to a tree.

Maybe he could communicate with the tree through drawings! Steve grabbed a pen off the top of his dresser, ripped a piece of paper from a nearby notebook, and drew the first thing that popped into his head. He didn't think while he did this; he just drew and drew.

When he finished his drawing, he stepped back and looked at it for a moment. It looked like some kind of pencil sharpener. Or maybe it was a very small raccoon holding a snowball.

Whatever it was, Steve went back to the window, held the drawing up to his mother's oak, and wondered what the hell he was doing.

10

"What the hell am I doing?" Steve muttered to himself as he stared into his refrigerator.

He was looking for something he could bring with him to eat for lunch. He was grateful to have learned that his wife was cancer-free, but with the fifty-four thousand he'd soon be spending to rub out the Pool Pisser, money was tight. With the exception of Pizza Munch on Wednesdays, Steve thought it would be a good idea to avoid eating out for the time being.

He discovered the large plastic container that Kelly used to pack the carrot salad. Steve opened the lid and took a whiff.

"Ugh," he said. He had always wished that his wife would get into the habit of making pizzas. Surely homemade pizza had something in it that could fight off Alzheimer's. And it would certainly taste a lot better than fucking carrots.

Steve walked back upstairs to the master bathroom to say goodbye to Kelly.

"I'm going to work now," Steve said through the door. "And I'm taking the carrot salad."

Steve actually had no intention of eating the salad. In fact, his plan was to dispose of it at his earliest opportunity. But he figured that as long as Kelly thought he was eating it that she would be happy and therefore less inclined to lock herself in the master bathroom again anytime soon.

The doorknob slowly turned and out walked Kelly.

"I'm glad you've come to your senses," she said.

"This from a woman who just locked herself in a bathroom over night," said Steve.

Kelly frowned. "I'm just making a joke," said Steve.

"You think Alzheimer's is a joke?"

"Jesus, Kelly, of course not. And neither is cancer. I'm glad neither of us has either." Steve pulled Kelly toward him and kissed her on the cheek.

Kelly knew that Steve was not always the easiest person to communicate with and she'd grown to accept that about him. She knew what a difficult upbringing he'd had, having been raised by a pharmacist who never allowed him to eat at diners or wear baseball gloves.

She still didn't like the idea that Steve didn't feel he could enjoy eating Pizza Munch with his wife present, but if he needed time to himself periodically, she decided she could accept that. Besides, he was now taking the carrot salad with him to work. The carrots would help prevent Steve from developing Alzheimer's, and at the end of the day, Kelly knew that was what was most important anyway.

She briefly considered bringing up her "Carrot Salad Thursdays" idea to Steve, but decided she didn't want to overwhelm him. So instead she gave Steve a peck on the lips and said, "You have a good day at work."

"I don't see how I couldn't! I've got carrot salad!" he said.

This time Kelly laughed at Steve's joke.

Then Steve walked into the bathroom and grabbed his bottle of cologne.

11

Kelly was glad that she and Steve were able to make peace before Steve went to work. She was fully prepared to stay in the bathroom for as long as it took, even if it meant missing her compliments class.

Kelly had been terrible at giving people compliments her entire life, so she decided to do something about it and signed up for an eight-week compliments intensive.

She was sick of using the excuse, *Nobody ever taught me how to give them.*

She was also working on *receiving* compliments because her instructor, Jennifer, picked up on the fact that Kelly was weak in that area as well.

"In western culture, sometimes receiving compliments can be just as difficult as giving them," Jennifer had said.

Kelly was now six weeks into the program and she had learned a great deal. She'd been trained to compliment people on their clothes, their shoes, their hairstyle, their smile, and even their math skills.

This class was also where Kelly met Eric. Eric was incredibly shy the first week of the program and Kelly didn't think he had any chance of making it through the entire eight weeks. She thought for sure that this class would eat him alive. But Eric surprised everyone as he quickly picked up on key compliment-giving techniques and masterfully put them to use.

By the third week, Eric and Kelly found themselves studying together outside of class. Kelly told Eric that since she was married she didn't think her husband would appreciate her bringing a male study partner home, so Kelly suggested they instead meet at a park.

"That's a great idea," said Eric. "You're great at brainstorming."

"Do you really feel that way?" said Kelly. "Or are you just paying me a compliment?"

Eric smiled. "I do feel that way *and* I'm paying you a compliment."

Kelly blushed. Of course he was just paying her a compliment. No harm, no foul. Jennifer had been dead-on with her assessment of Kelly being weak in the compliment-receiving area. Lord knows Kelly rarely received compliments from Steve anymore.

She was nervous as she entered the building for today's compliments class. She was nervous because the last time she saw Eric was two days ago in the park and that afternoon he presented Kelly with a flower.

"What am I supposed to do with this?" she asked. "I'm married."

"I know," said Eric. "But I saw the flower and it reminded me of you."

Kelly was suspicious, but rather than get defensive she did her best to employ the compliment techniques that she had been studying the past several weeks.

"Eric," she said, "you said the flower reminds you of me and flowers are generally considered to be pretty, so I recognize that you have just given me a compliment. I accept that compliment and I thank you for it."

Eric smiled.

"I would now like to give you a compliment," she said. "You are a very thoughtful person."

Then Kelly and Eric made out on the park bench they were

sitting on. They made out hard. Kelly bit Eric's lip so severely at one point that it drew blood and they briefly had to stop to make sure Eric was going to be okay. After they determined that Eric was fit for more making out, they continued to go at it until their tongues went numb.

Kelly and Eric then composed themselves, complimented each other on their kissing skills, and went their separate ways.

That was two days ago and they hadn't spoken since.

Kelly sat down in a chair and waited for class to start. Jennifer walked into the classroom and told everyone that she had an announcement to make.

"I received a note from Eric," she said. "He has decided to drop the course. He said in his note that he found this class to be extremely helpful but he feels he has gone as far as he can with it and would like to use his time to pursue other endeavors. He said he will miss each and every one of us, especially those of us who reminded him of a flower... whatever that means."

Kelly couldn't tell if she was having a panic attack or if she was depressed. She felt incredibly sad, but her heart also started beating rapidly. She did her best to breathe through it.

Jennifer went on to talk about the pitfalls of thinking one has mastered the art of the compliment and wrongly believing that one did not require further education on the subject. She then decided to make that the topic of the days' lesson. She wrote *Compliment Overconfidence: The True Enemy* on the chalkboard and lectured for three hours about how if you didn't work at it every single day, your confidence-giving and receiving skills would slowly wither away.

Then she reminded everyone that the final exam was only a week away, and students would be required to score at least seventy percent in order to obtain their certificates.

Even through her mixture of anxiety and depression, Kelly was able to see that this information about compliment overconfidence was incredibly valuable. The only information that would have been even more valuable to her in that moment would have been the exact whereabouts of Eric.

12

Steve was a bit of a jerk. Depending on whom you asked, some people would say he was a "big jerk." Others would say he was "kind of a jerk" and still others would insist that he was "the biggest jerk" they'd ever met.

But Steve hadn't always been a jerk. In fact, at one point in his life Steve had been a lumberjack.

By the time Steve turned eighteen, his relationship with his father had deteriorated to such an extent that Steve decided to run off and eat at diners and become a lumberjack.

He started eating at diners because diners were of course taboo in the eyes of his father and he wanted to rub the old man's nose in it. He decided to become a lumberjack because that was a profession that Steve felt was as far away from being a pharmacist as one could get.

Steve had no intention of doing anything in his life remotely similar to what his father did. So that meant no career in pharmaceuticals and certainly no career involving little wooden boats.

Steve had always loved trees, or at the very least, he had always loved that thirty-foot oak in his backyard, so he thought that a career working with trees made sense, even if it meant chopping the trees down.

He looked at a map one day, located the forest that was the farthest from his father's house, and set off to get a job there. He ate at diners along the way and discovered that he was actually really good at eating at them. No waitress ever asked him if he was a first-timer and as near as Steve could tell, he never once made a rookie mistake. Eating at diners was something he took to naturally and he hoped that he would find himself to be equally gifted in the lumberjack field.

When Steve finally arrived at his destination, he walked into the logging company's trailer, asked for the person in charge, and told him he was "ready to get a choppin'."

The owner of the logging company was a wiry man who wore a cowboy hat. He informed Steve that Steve was already talking to the person in charge and he asked Steve what made him think he was qualified for this type of work.

Steve cited his fantastic reflexes as well as his ability to play baseball without a glove.

"Play baseball without a glove?" the owner asked. "What the hell does that have to do with anything?"

"It means I'm tough," said Steve. "It means I've got what it takes to bring a tree to its knees. It means I'm not a pine rider. It means THE PINE RIDES ME."

The owner had no idea what this kid was yammering about with all this talk of riding the pine and getting ridden by pine. Still, there was something about Steve's moxie that he liked. In a way, Steve reminded him of himself at that age and the enthusiasm that he once had for the logging industry. So what if the kid was a little funny in the head? Hell, you had to be a little funny in the head to get into this line of work in the first place. In that regard it wasn't unlike becoming a skydiving instructor or a pharmacist.

Plus, business was booming. They couldn't move the logs fast enough. If nothing else, he could hire Steve as an office assistant. Steve could take out the garbage, answer the phone, and help break up fights when they arose.

"You're hired," said the owner.

"Really?" said Steve. "I'm going to be a lumberjack?"

"Lumberjack?" laughed the owner. "You gotta earn that. No, you'll be doing administrative work."

The offer was a bit of a blow to Steve's ego. He had been mentally prepared to take up lumberjacking immediately. However, he didn't have any other job offers at the moment, he was in the middle of nowhere, he was running low on cash, and he wasn't about to call home to ask his father for money.

Besides, what was wrong with doing administrative work in a forest? You had to start somewhere.

"What's the pay?" said Steve.

"Not much."

"Where do I sleep?"

"Outside."

"Just outside on the ground?"

"Outside in a tent. There's tents in the warehouse out back. Go grab one at the end of the day."

"When do I start?"

"You're on the clock right now."

"What do you want me to do?"

The owner looked out the window and saw two of his best sawyers exchanging blows.

"Get out there and break up that fight before they kill each other."

13

Steve had told Kelly he was in for a busy day at work. In actuality, there was no job for Steve to go to. He'd been fired from his job as a headhunter a month ago for accepting bribes and not telling anyone about it.

Steve was in charge of job placement for nightclub security guards. Nightclub security guard was a coveted position for many strapping young men as it provided them with a power that they couldn't find at other jobs, since it was ultimately up to them to decide who did or did not get to enter the club.

The nightclub security guard jobs generally also came with one free meal a night and the opportunity to interact with beautiful young women who might not otherwise give these men the time of day.

The bribes Steve received were never all that much—twenty-five dollars here, a hundred there—but the bribes covered Steve's annual gym membership, paid for his meals at Pizza Munch, and helped him pad his otherwise mediocre salary.

Trouble arose when one of the strapping young men who'd bribed Steve by giving him thirty-five dollars grew frustrated with Steve's inability to place him as a security guard at one of the town's nightclubs.

The young man left a series of voicemails for Steve that were never returned, so eventually the young man went over Steve's head and spoke to Steve's boss. He told Steve's boss about the bribe and that Steve hadn't returned his calls.

Steve's boss wasn't upset to learn that Steve accepted bribes. As far as Steve's boss knew, everyone at their office accepted bribes, but he *was* upset that Steve hadn't shared any of the bribes with him.

So Steve was let go, and Steve's boss set his sights on finding a replacement for Steve who would instinctively know to share his or her bribes with the higher-ups.

Steve couldn't be bothered with that memory today, though. He had one thing on his mind this morning and that was to nail the Pool Pisser.

So Steve went to the gym. He parked in the gym's underground parking lot, dumped the carrot salad in the garbage by the gym's elevator, brought the plastic container back to his car (he knew Kelly would appreciate him saving it), and then rode the elevator up to the gym's lobby.

He then headed straight to the pool to observe the people using it and to see if any of them might make a false move that would reveal to him who the true culprit was.

In order to get to the pool, Steve had to pass by the office of the gym's manager, Chester Rawlings. Chester Rawlings was a former competitive swimmer and had now served as the gym's manager for nearly a decade.

When Steve and Chester first met, they made the connection that they were the same age and that revelation initially bonded the two men.

"Not every day you meet someone the same age as you," said Steve.

"No, sir," said Chester. "This is something special here."

Both men were now fifty-two, but being the same age was no longer enough to sustain their previously friendly relationship.

Things started to go south three months ago when Steve first became suspicious of someone urinating in the pool. He brought the matter up to Chester and he found Chester to be surprisingly unsympathetic to his concern.

"Not much we can do about it," said Chester. "Studies show that one in five Americans have admitted to peeing in the pool. And those are just the ones that cop to it. I'd say that it's really more like one in three. Maybe even one in two. No way we can monitor that amount of urine. No way."

"You can do something to the water," said Steve. "You can put a chemical in there so that when someone pisses, the water changes color."

"That's an invasion of privacy," said Chester. "That's not going to happen."

"So you're *protecting* the pissers now?" Steve was fuming. "There's something incredibly backwards about that. Why do they get all the rights?"

Chester then suggested to Steve that he go home and cool off. Steve took Chester's advice. They were the same age after all, and that's what two men of the same age do: they take each other's advice.

But something continued to bother Steve whenever he used the pool. He could sense that he was surrounded by urine and he didn't pay good money to belong to a gym only to be immersed in piss.

With Chester having made it clear that he would not aid Steve in his quest to find the miscreant, Steve decided to take matters into his own hands by asking people who were in the pool at the same time as him if they ever used the pool as a bathroom.

You better believe Chester got some complaints about Steve and he eventually had to call Steve into his office to lay down the law.

"Steve, listen," said Chester. "You need to understand something. You need to understand that pools and urine go hand in hand. Always have, always will. You can not have one without the other."

"Bullshit!" said Steve. "Where I grew up, no one ever pissed in the pool!"

"I highly doubt that," said Chester. "I think you just weren't paying attention then. And if I were you, I'd stop paying so much attention to it now. You're scaring your fellow gym members."

"Good!" yelled Steve. "Let's watch 'em squirm. Now that they know I'm on to them, maybe they'll rat each other out. Let's see if they can take the heat!"

"No!" said Chester. "This is not how gyms work! You are to leave the other gym members alone and that is final."

"Huh," said Steve. "So that's how it is? Doesn't even matter that we're the same age anymore. You're just going to take their side."

"Are you playing the same-age card?" yelled Chester.

Steve smirked. "I guess maybe I am."

"Get out of my office and clean up your act or you can switch gyms for all I care!" yelled Chester.

That was the last time Steve and Chester had spoken. Since that exchange, Steve cleaned up his act. Or at least, he let Chester think that. Steve was of course working behind the scenes, collecting intel and observing the gym members, waiting for one of them to slip up just once so he could pounce.

Steve was now tiptoeing past Chester's office. He peered inside to see Chester talking to someone on the phone. Steve did feel bad about having played the same-age card a while back, but at the same time, in a situation like this, you had to be cutthroat. You had to know who was on your side and who was an enemy. And it had become clear to Steve that Chester was not on his side, which meant that he had to be an enemy.

Steve couldn't recall ever having been at odds with someone the same age as him. It just didn't happen. The same-age bond had always carried his same-age friendships through the darkest of times.

As he passed by Chester's office, it occurred to Steve that perhaps Chester had lied to him about his age. Maybe Chester wasn't fifty-two after all. And if he'd lied about his age, what else might he have lied to Steve about?

Could it be that *Chester* was the Pool Pisser?

Steve couldn't believe he'd never considered the possibility before. Just then his phone rang. He recognized the number. It was one of the men from the previous night. Maybe he had an update for him—some type of progress report.

Steve didn't want to risk Chester overhearing the call, so he walked outside before accepting it.

"Talk to me," said Steve.

14

"I like your dog," said Kelly. "It looks really smart."

Kelly was sitting on a bench at the park where she and Eric regularly met and was in the process of paying a compliment to a complete stranger. There was an acronym that Jennifer—Kelly's compliments instructor—drilled into her students' heads from day one.

That acronym was A.B.C.

It stood for "Always Be Complimenting."

Jennifer insisted that everyone in her class had to compliment at least ten different people every day and at least eight of those people had to be people that they didn't know.

"Thanks," said the stranger. "He's actually kind of dumb for a Pomeranian but I love him to death."

"Does he have Alzheimer's?" said Kelly.

"Excuse me?" said the stranger.

"Alzheimer's," Kelly repeated. "Two Scotties on my husband's side of the family suffered from it."

"I didn't know dogs could get Alzheimer's," said the stranger.

"Dogs can get all kinds of things," said Kelly.

The stranger walked away, unsure of what to make of Kelly's Alzheimer's comments.

Kelly was off her game today and she knew it. She was usually much better at complimenting people, but she was distracted.

Where the fuck was Eric? That son of a bitch. Fucking men and their fucking disappearing acts. She thought that Eric was different. She *knew* that Eric was different. If she hadn't known he was different she wouldn't have made out with him in the first place.

Kelly was married after all and she wasn't about to jeopardize a perfectly uninspired marriage to make out with some guy who was going to flake on her after one round of tonsil hockey.

But that's exactly what she'd done! She'd made out with a typical man. She'd made out with a man who wanted to run away as soon as things got too intense. *That fucking running-away-mother-fucking son of a bitch.* Eric could get Alzheimer's for all Kelly cared. The fucker deserved it.

Kelly caught herself. She knew she had to stop this negative train of thought immediately. Jennifer always said that one negative thought negated three compliments. Kelly had already lost track of how many negative thoughts she'd just had and there was no way she was going to go back and count them because she knew she wouldn't be pleased with the result.

So she simply made up her mind to stop thinking negative thoughts about Eric for the time being.

When things had been better between Kelly and Eric, Eric had suggested that they exchange phone numbers. Kelly shot that idea down, not wanting to get too familiar too soon. Now she was kicking herself because she had no idea how to get a hold of Eric. Even though she was furious with him at the moment, she still wanted to at least know that he was okay. What if Eric didn't really want to quit the class? What if someone had forced him to write that letter against his will? Eric had shown so much promise as a complimenter; it seemed incredibly peculiar to Kelly that he could give it up just like that.

She had envisioned Eric as the type of person who could have a lucrative career as he traveled the world, giving inspiring seminars to stadiums full of would-be complimenters. He could perhaps start his own compliments classes and have them located in cities from Honolulu to Hamburg. She had also envisioned herself traveling to these cities with Eric, joining him on stage in triumph, and then returning to their hotel room where they would pop a bottle of champagne and compliment each other until sunrise.

Sure, Kelly had only been holding onto this fantasy for a couple of weeks, but it was gone now. There would be no seminars, no world travel, and no romantic compliment sessions in international cities.

There still could be champagne, though. Even if she wasn't drinking it with Eric, she could at least drink it by herself.

It was 1:30 p.m. on a weekday, which wasn't normally a time of day when Kelly would consider a drink. Actually, she rarely drank at all anymore. But now she was craving champagne—an entire bottle of it, in fact.

Kelly got up from the park bench and made her way to her car. As she walked, she wondered what had gotten into her lately. She'd beaten her husband with a magazine last night, something she would normally never do. She'd also lockedherself in a bathroom. She couldn't remember having done that since she'd had a quarrel with a friend when she was nine years old. Now here she was thinking negative thoughts about Eric and strongly entertaining the idea of drinking an entire bottle of champagne by herself—on a weekday afternoon, no less.

No, Kelly was not herself right now.

As she approached her car, she found two teenagers leaning against it, each smoking a cigarette. The teenagers weren't hoodlums. They weren't drunk, and they weren't looking for trouble. In fact, if someone had told Kelly that this was the very first cigarette either of these teenagers had ever smoked, she would have believed it. These teenagers were of the nerdy variety and were obviously smoking in an attempt to look "cool," although clearly neither of them had any chance of ever attaining any kind of cool lifestyle.

"This is my car," Kelly said to them.

The teenagers sprang from the car, as if they'd been zapped by a cattle prod.

"Sorry," said the boy.

Although nerdy, the teenagers were not unattractive. The boy had wavy hair and icy blue eyes. The girl had perfect skin and a nose that would most likely never require plastic surgery.

There were several things that Kelly could have complimented either of the teenagers on, and it would have behooved her to offer them compliments since she was still very far from meeting her daily compliments quota.

Kelly didn't offer either of them a compliment, though.

Instead she said, "You both deserve to be shot."

Then she got in her car and drove to a liquor store.

15

It took four years, but Steve finally worked his way up to the rank of lumberjack.

In those four years leading up to his promotion, Steve answered a lot of phone calls, took out a lot of garbage, and broke up a lot of fights.

He also slept outside in a tent, on the ground, for two of those four years. Eventually he was invited to sleep in a cabin with the other loggers, but Steve often times found himself choosing to sleep outside in his tent when the noise from the loggers' snoring got to be too loud.

Before being crowned a lumberjack, Steve did the things that lumberjacks did in preparation for when the big day came: he grew a beard, he ate a shitload of pancakes, and he wore a lot of flannel shirts.

He also occasionally wrote home to his father. Steve decided it was fair that he write his father twice a year to at least let him know that he was alive.

A typical letter from Steve to his father during those days read something like this:

Dear Dad,
I hope you are well. I'm doing well.

I'm still working with trees and I'm still loving it.
The pine continues to ride me.
The pine will always ride me.
I hope you and your little wooden boats are happy.
I'm happy.
Regards,
Steve

One time the owner noticed Steve writing a letter to his father.

"Whatcha writing there?"

"A letter to my dad."

"That's great. Maybe I'll write a letter to my dad, too."

But the owner never wrote a letter to his father. Not even once. The owner's father never had any idea what was going on in his son's life.

Steve even approached the owner at one point and offered to write a letter to the owner's father on the owner's behalf.

"It's a good thing to write letters to your father," said Steve, "even if they're a pharmacist."

The owner went on to explain to Steve that his father was not a pharmacist and the reason he did not write him letters was…

was…

When it came down to it, the owner couldn't think of any reason *not* to write to his father and he couldn't think of any reason not to have Steve write to his father on his behalf. But instead of relenting and simply letting Steve write the letter, the owner decided to create a diversion and that diversion consisted of promoting Steve to lumberjack, right there on the spot.

"You're kidding!" said Steve.

"Well, you've put in your time answering phones, taking out the garbage, and breaking up fights. You've done great work and you've earned it."

Steve was beside himself with excitement. He wrapped his arms around the owner and gave him one hell of a hug. It was the type of father-son hug you would see in a movie, except that Steve was not the owner's son and the owner was not Steve's father and neither man had seen a movie since they went into the logging business.

Steve worked as a lumberjack for all of four days.

On that fourth day, Steve returned to the cabin where the loggers slept and came across a few of his fellow lumberjacks who were enjoying some beers and carousing.

Steve thought that looked like a good idea—to have a beer and carouse. So he joined them.

One of the loggers was named Brad. Steve and Brad actually got along pretty well. Like Steve, Brad had also run away from his father to pursue a career as a lumberjack. On one occasion, a couple years back, Brad had even brought Steve pancakes when Steve was sick with a cold and was sleeping outside in his tent during a period when the snoring of the loggers in the cabin had been excessively loud.

On this day, however—Steve's fourth as a lumberjack—when he saw Brad, he couldn't believe his eyes.

Brad was holding a tiny wooden boat.

"Excuse me, Brad," said Steve, "is that a tiny wooden boat?"

"Sure is," said Brad.

Steve did his best to compose himself but he felt a rage building up inside of him. He hadn't been exposed to a tiny wooden boat since he was living at home with his father and he could feel himself start to lose control.

"But... what is it doing here?" said Steve.

"I made it," said Brad. "Pretty cool, huh?"

"Can I see it?" said Steve.

"Sure," said Brad, handing Steve the boat.

Steve ran his fingers over the boat. Not only was the boat tiny and wooden, but it was also well-made, and that pissed Steve off even more.

"Why did you do this?" said Steve.

"Excuse me?"

"Why did you fucking DO THIS?"

Now Brad was starting to get irritated. Why was Steve asking him all these questions and why was he directing all this hostility toward his boat?

"Because we're in a forest and we're surrounded by wood and I used some of that wood to make a tiny wooden boat. That's why I fucking did it. Now can I have my boat back?"

Steve did not give the boat back to Brad. Instead he attacked him with it. Brad had not anticipated getting attacked by someone using his tiny wooden boat as a weapon against him and as a result, Steve got in some terrific licks, breaking Brad's nose with the first of those licks and breaking his jaw with either the second, third, or fourth lick. (It was difficult to determine exactly which of the licks broke Brad's jaw, but it was one of them.)

Most people in Brad's position would have been knocked unconscious after being struck by those licks, but Brad was entering his fourth *year* as a lumberjack and he sure as hell wasn't going to allow himself to get beaten up by some guy who had only been a lumberjack for four *days*.

So Brad fought back. He wrestled the boat away from Steve and then started hitting Steve with it. Then Steve knocked the boat out of Brad's hand and got in a few more licks himself. Then Brad returned the favor with a few licks of his own.

They went back and forth like this as the other lumberjacks stood around and watched the two men swap licks. The problem was there was currently no one designated to break up fights. Everyone knew that up until four days ago Steve was in charge of breaking up fights and unfortunately the owner had not yet had the opportunity to hire someone to perform Steve's old duties.

During this period, the owner had to take out the garbage and answer the phones himself and those added responsibilities, on top of his normal responsibilities of running the company, made it very difficult for him to break up fights in a timely manner.

So Steve and Brad continued to wallop each other until they fell to the ground in exhaustion.

Steve must have passed out because when he came to, the

owner was standing over him.

"Steve," said the owner, "we need to talk about your future."

"My future?" said Steve, as he gingerly rolled onto his side and rubbed his throbbing head.

"Yes," said the owner, "because it isn't here."

16

"No update? What do you mean you don't have an update?" said Steve.

Steve was standing outside the gym, talking on the phone to one of the men he'd met the night before at Pizza Munch.

"How can we have an update when you didn't give us anything to go on?" said the man. "You didn't give us any kind of description of who this person is. You didn't even give us the address of the gym."

"Jesus Christ," said Steve. "Aren't you guys supposed to think to ask me that stuff? This is my first time doing this. I can't be expected to know everything."

"All the same," said the man, "your failure to provide us with the proper information has caused us to lose valuable time and we're now going to need seventy-two hundred up front."

"What????"

"Yes. We're going to need an additional eight hundred dollars to get this thing going."

"How the hell are you coming up with these numbers?"

The second man grabbed the phone and started talking to Steve.

"If you want us to catch this guy, just do what we fucking say."

"Jesus Christ," said Steve. "I can't believe I wasted two good lemonades on you guys. This is bullshit!"

"Do what we fucking say," said the second man. "Otherwise we can't guarantee this thing will go smoothly."

Steve considered this for a moment. "So you're saying if I give you another eight hundred up front, you *can* guarantee it will go smoothly?"

"No. I'm saying that if you *don't* give us the additional eight hundred, I can almost guarantee that it *won't* go smoothly."

"This is bullshit," said Steve. "Bullshit, bullshit, bullshit."

As Steve explained to the men what he thought of their proposal, Chester Rawlings walked out to the courtyard where Steve was standing and lit a cigarette.

It certainly was odd that Chester Rawlings—a former competitive swimmer-turned-gym manager—would smoke, but he did. And he chose to smoke outside the gym's front entrance three to five times a day.

None of the gym members ever complained about Chester's smoking. Chester was well-liked and the majority of the people who went to his gym understood that nobody's perfect and if Chester's lone vice was to smoke in front of the gym three to five times a day, then so be it.

Chester nodded to Steve as he lit up. It wasn't a friendly nod or an unfriendly nod. It was simply a nod. Steve was standing out of earshot of Chester, but he moved farther away from him to ensure Chester wouldn't overhear anything.

"All right," Steve whispered into the phone, "you want a description? Black male. Early fifties. Goes by the name of Chester Rawlings. He wears gold wire rim glasses. I'd guess he's 6'2", two hundred pounds. He's the manager of my gym and he's a smoker. The address of the gym is 5000 Johnson. There's your description and there's your location. You happy now?"

"What about the others?" said the second man. "You said you had it narrowed down to fifteen people."

"No," said Steve. "That was yesterday. Yesterday I had it narrowed down to fifteen people or thereabouts. But today I've got it narrowed down to one person and I just told you who he is. So when can you take care of this?"

"Depends."

"Depends on what?"

"Depends on when you get us that eight hundred."

"Oh, for the love of fuck."

The second man handed the phone back to the first man who explained to Steve that he needed to leave an envelope containing eight hundred dollars under the garbage can in front of the Pizza Munch. The drop had to take place by midnight that evening and the men would contact Steve after they retrieved the money.

Steve suggested that the three of them just meet at the Pizza Munch parking lot at a mutually convenient time, but the men told Steve that this was how it had to be done if there was to be any chance of this thing going smoothly.

Steve reluctantly agreed, but made it known that he would be making the drop out of protest. He then hung up and considered waiting for Chester Rawlings to go back inside before he walked back into the gym to take the elevator down to his car.

"Jesus Christ," said Steve as he watched Chester light up a second cigarette. It was obvious Chester wasn't going anywhere anytime soon. Steve was not a patient person, so rather than wait it out, he decided to just head back into the gym, even if it meant an awkward moment with his former friend.

"Hello," said Steve as he approached Chester.

"Hello," said Chester.

"Lovely day," said Steve.

"Sure is," said Chester. "Not going for a swim, are you?"

"Wouldn't think of it," said Steve. "Not as long as that pissing bandit is still on the loose."

Chester smiled and took a drag from his cigarette.

Steve entered the gym and rode the elevator down to the garage. He got in his car and pulled out his bottle of cologne he'd retrieved from the bathroom earlier that morning.

He splashed some cologne on his face. Man, he loved that

sensation.

He then thought about how he was about to pay two men fifty-four thousand dollars to kill his former friend. He wondered if it was worth it.

Then he stopped wondering if it was worth it, grabbed the manila envelope that was under the passenger seat, counted out eight hundred dollars, and started to make his way to Pizza Munch.

17

Kelly was home, drinking champagne. She'd purchased two bottles. When she'd entered the liquor store, she had intended to buy only one bottle, but then she noticed that the store was running a special, where if you bought one bottle of champagne, the second bottle was three percent off. Kelly knew this wasn't exactly an offer she couldn't refuse, but at the same time she felt she might want to drink two bottles of champagne and if she could save three percent off the second bottle in the process, then why not live a little?

She brought the bottles up to the counter and although she wasn't really in the mood to compliment anyone, she summoned the strength to say something positive to the clerk, who was also the owner of the liquor store.

"This is a great store," she said. "I really like your specials."

"Listen," said the owner, "I know our specials suck but I could really do without the sarcasm."

"No," said Kelly, "I really mean it."

"Uh huh. I bet you do."

"I'm sorry. I was just trying to pay you a compliment."

"Well, what say you just *pay* for the champagne and we'll call it a day," said the owner.

Kelly was replaying this exchange in her mind as she sat alone at the kitchen table, drinking champagne straight from the bottle.

This was the first time she'd had someone reject one of her compliments. She wasn't sure if she would still be given credit for having complimented the owner of the liquor store since he had clearly not accepted it. Either way, she was not going to meet her compliments quota for the day, as she had no intention of leaving the house in her drunken state.

She would also have to talk to Jennifer at her next class (which would also be her *final* class) to find out how to handle people who reject compliments. As she thought about it, she became somewhat irritated that Jennifer hadn't already addressed this type of situation. Compliment rejections were probably fairly commonplace, and wasn't Jennifer planning on equipping her students with the necessary skills to deal with a scenario of this sort?

Kelly went to the refrigerator, popped open the second bottle of champagne, took a swig, and then grabbed one of the phone books that was sitting on top of the fridge. She sat back down, opened the phone book, and pulled out the flower that Eric had given her the last time they were together.

She knew she couldn't display the flower in a vase out in the open as Steve might ask her where the flower came from. Of course, since Steve paid so little attention to her these days, and since he'd never cared for flowers anyway, she knew the odds of him suspecting anything were incredibly slim. Still, why take the chance?

So she'd decided to press the flower in the phone book instead. She sat with the flattened flower, twirling it in her hand. It was a violet, and since Kelly hadn't eaten all day and since she knew violets were edible, she popped it in her mouth and swallowed it, stem and all.

She then pulled out her laptop and went to a message board and started leaving random compliments on people's posts like it was nobody's business. Eric might have driven her to drink and to eat the flower he'd given her, but he sure as hell wasn't going to prevent her from reaching her daily compliments quota.

She exploded with a flood of compliments, writing anything from *Your knowledge of politics is very impressive* to *It must take a lot of guts to discuss the mating habits of cows so openly.*

On one particularly heated message board she wrote, *You sure have a knack for telling people to go fuck themselves! I wish I had an ounce of your talent.* :)

Her compliments flurry concluded, Kelly shut her laptop and took another swig from the second bottle of champagne. But this time when she took a swig, no champagne came out. Had she already finished both bottles?

"Guess I should have bought three," she said with a laugh.

With no champagne left to drink, and with no further compliments left to give, Kelly figured it was as good a time as any to take a nap.

18

Steve's final days as a lumberjack were not particularly happy ones. Nor were they the most comfortable, as Steve received no medical attention for the injuries he sustained from his dust-up with Brad.

In the lumberjack world, there was an unwritten rule that if you were the one who started a fight, you didn't get medical attention. The owner let Steve know that every witness he'd spoken to said Steve had clearly initiated the fight, and therefore Steve would have to pay for his hospital bills on his own.

"We're gonna cover Brad on this one," said the owner. "In fact he's already at the hospital getting the finest medical attention any lumberjack could hope for."

Steve and the owner were sitting in the owner's trailer, just like the first day they met.

"I'm pretty busted up," said Steve. "I don't know if I have broken ribs, but it feels like I might. I'm really in a lot of pain."

"Well, maybe you shouldn't have attacked a fellow lumberjack for making wooden boats. Then we wouldn't even have to be here to discuss this."

"Well, maybe you should have assigned someone else to break up fights besides me!" yelled Steve. "Then maybe things wouldn't have gotten so out of hand!" It pained him to yell since his ribs were so sore and since he couldn't feel one side of his face, but he yelled anyway. "Maybe you could have assigned an understudy to break up fights in my absence or in the event that I was ill or in the event like this one where *I* was the one in the fight. Are you saying I was supposed to break up *my own fight?* That's preposterous!"

"Listen," said the owner, "I've seen a lot of fights in my day, and they usually stem from a guy eating another guy's pancakes without permission or a guy shaving another guy's beard off when he was passed out drunk. Those are the kinds of fights we can tolerate. But we cannot tolerate fights over wooden boats. It's just not natural."

"I'm sorry," said Steve. "I didn't know the sight of a wooden boat would affect me like that. My dad used to paint tiny wooden boats when I was a kid. He did it because of the tremendous stress he was under as a pharmacist. I've told you I've never gotten along well with my dad, and when I saw that tiny wooden boat, I just snapped."

"Steve, up to this point, you've been a real asset here. A *real* asset. And I completely empathize with you getting angry when you think about your dad. I admire that you write him letters a couple of times a year. I can't imagine writing my dad a letter. He's so old now; I don't know that he can read anyway. I think he's at that age where your brain sort of naturally gets fucked up and there's nothing anyone can do about it. Be that as it may, I've spoken to the guys, and they all want you gone. I'm going to have to transfer you."

Just as there was an unwritten rule in the lumberjack world about not receiving medical attention if you were the one who started a fight, there was also an unwritten rule that a transfer was the worst possible fate a lumberjack could receive.

No lumberjack ever wanted to be known as a "transferer." It was a label one could never live down, no matter how skilled of a lumberjack one was.

In that moment, Steve knew his lumberjack days were over.

"I wish you'd reconsider," said Steve.

"My hands are tied," said the owner.

"Well, I'm not going out without a fight," said Steve.

"I didn't think you would," said the owner. "They're waiting for you."

Steve slowly stood up, grunting as he held his ribs, and shook the owner's hand. He looked out the window to see the entire lumberjack crew standing outside the trailer, waiting to kick his ass.

When a lumberjack was given a transfer, he had one of two options. The first option was he could accept the transfer and report for duty at the company where he was reassigned. If the lumberjack chose that option, he would also forever be known as a pansy. The second option was to retire, fight everyone in the company at once and in the process get the shit beaten out of you, but at the same time retain some semblance of pride.

Ninety-nine percent of lumberjacks with any self-respect chose the second option.

As Steve hobbled out of the trailer to meet his ass kicking head-on, the owner spoke up.

"Steve," he said.

Steve turned around.

"You were a lumberjack for four days. That's four days longer than most people can say they were a lumberjack. Never forget that."

"Thanks," said Steve. "And remember it's never too late to write your father a letter, even if he's at an age where his brain's fucked up and there's nothing anyone can do about it."

The owner nodded and Steve walked out the door to get his ass kicked and start the next chapter of his journey.

Steve was twenty-two years old.

19

Steve was holding the empty plastic container that had held his wife's carrot salad as he let himself into the house. He'd told Kelly he had a big day ahead of him, and as it turned out, it ended up being a very big day indeed.

For one thing, he'd identified who the Pool Pisser was. It was Chester Rawlings. And he was so sure it was Chester Rawlings that he was willing to pay fifty-four thousand dollars to have him knocked off.

The two men had requested an additional eight hundred up front to carry out that task, which Steve had initially thought was unfair. But the more he thought about it, the more he felt it wasn't such a bad deal after all, especially considering how Steve was originally going to pay them half up front. Even with him now paying them seventy-two hundred up front, that was still only thirteen percent of the entire fifty-four thousand.

"In my next life, I'll be an agent," Steve said to himself. Steve believed in life after death and he believed that his primo negotiating skills were most likely inherited from a past life. How else could one explain Steve's uncanny knack for wheeling and dealing? "Yes, I will be an agent and I'll get my shoes shined three times a week!"

Steve had made the drop earlier in the day. He left the eight hundred under the garbage can in front of the Pizza Munch, just as they had asked. He even paper-clipped the bills together to make sure none of them blew away in case there was any unexpected wind.

And since he was already at Pizza Munch, he decided to walk inside and treat himself to a pizza.

He ordered a medium deep dish supreme, then sat back and relaxed. Pizza Munch truly was the best environment for one to relax. He was there in the late afternoon, too, so he'd missed the lunch rush and the dinner crowd hadn't shown up yet. It felt like he had the whole place to himself. He sat there with his thoughts, thinking about his lumberjack days and dreaming about all the swimming he'd be doing once Chester was no longer around.

Normally Steve only ate at Pizza Munch on Wednesdays, and normally only after a workout at the gym, when his metabolism was high. He didn't let it bother him that he was eating there two days in a row. In a way, he was celebrating and he could always go to the gym two times tomorrow to make up for not going today.

The server brought Steve his pizza and dished Steve's first slice onto his plate. Steve loved this Pizza Munch tradition. Steve had never seen this young woman before. He chalked it up to his not normally being at Pizza Munch on Thursdays. Maybe she only worked on Thursdays.

Whoever she was, she certainly was pretty. She had full lips, almond brown eyes, and just the right amount of freckles on her cheeks. Steve wished the Pizza Munch uniforms were a little more flattering so he could see more of her figure, but he definitely liked what he was able to see. If he had to guess, Steve would have said she was around seventeen or eighteen years of age.

"Can I ask you something?" Steve said to the girl.

"Sure," she said.

"I look pretty good for fifty-two, yeah?"

"Oh, sure you do, sir."

"I thought so," said Steve. "I exercise. That helps a lot. Do you exercise?"

"Not really," said the girl.

"That's okay," said Steve. "You've got time."

"Can I get you anything else?"

"My wife used to be a waitress," said Steve. "She didn't like it all that much. Do you like it?"

"It's alright," said the girl.

"Yeah, you don't love it, though. That's okay. Not everyone's meant to waitress long-term. At least you get to waitress at Pizza Munch. Things could be a lot worse."

The young woman smiled and walked off to help another table.

Steve finished his pizza, left the young server a generous tip, and then left the restaurant. On his way to his car, he stopped by the garbage can, bent down to pretend to tie his shoe, and made sure the money was still there. It was. He considered calling the men to let them know he'd made the drop, but he figured that might make him look like an amateur. If they'd wanted him to confirm the drop, they would have said something.

So Steve got in his car and drove around for three hours, killing time until it was 6 p.m., and then he went home.

It wasn't unusual for Steve to drive around for hours on end these days. He really didn't have much to do during the day ever since he got fired for not sharing his bribes. He still hadn't told Kelly about his termination. He didn't want her to worry. One of Kelly's greatest fears in life was having to wait tables again. He didn't want her to think that money was tight and that she might have to go back to serving. He knew that he'd land a new job soon enough; he just couldn't focus on that right now while there was a guy urinating in the pool at the gym.

Once he eliminated the culprit—even though it would leave him penniless in the process—he knew he would finally be able to think again and then he'd be able to give his full attention to finding a job.

There were plenty of companies out there looking for fifty-two-year-olds with Steve's skill set. He was outgoing, he looked good for his age, and he could appreciate a quality pizza. What wasn't to like?

Steve continued to mentally review his positive attributes as he entered his house.

"Honey, I'm home!"

Steve normally *never* said anything like that, but he was in a great mood, with his belly full of Pizza Munch and the knowledge that Chester Rawlings wasn't long for this world. Maybe he'd even take Kelly out for a nice dinner and a glass of champagne.

"Babe, that carrot salad was *de*-licious," said Steve as he walked into the kitchen.

He found Kelly passed out at the kitchen table. There were two empty champagne bottles next to her and it appeared that Kelly—or perhaps a wild animal—had ripped apart a phone book, balled up the pages, and hurled them all over the kitchen.

Someone had also written on the refrigerator, in what appeared to be lipstick:

I ♥ E

Steve was not pleased by what he saw.

"*Since when do we have a phone book?*" he yelled.

20

Eric had enrolled in the compliments class to get laid. He hadn't been laid in some time, and he wasn't a fan of internet dating sites or social media apps or bars or hair salons or wherever it was that people were meeting these days and getting laid.

However, when he came across the flyer at the coffee shop that was advertising an eight-week compliments intensive, he figured that class would be the perfect place for him to score.

Eric's wife had died three years ago in a freak swing set accident. Eric was of course devastated by her passing, but when she died, they were going through a rough patch in their marriage. They weren't communicating very much and they definitely weren't sleeping together.

Eric shared some of this during his wife's eulogy, when he said, "My wife and I went through many ups and downs during our marriage, and unfortunately, most of those times were 'downs.' If I'm being completely honest with everyone here today, I must admit I can't recall what she looked like naked. That's how long it had been since we were last intimate. If I had a gun held to my head and was forced to identify her nude body in a lineup, I'm afraid I wouldn't be able to do it. In that hypothetical situation, I would probably end up getting shot. Still, she was a remarkable woman, and for the most part, I was honored to be her husband."

After the funeral, Eric did his best to get on with his life. He bought a plant and one of his colleagues suggested he name a star in the sky after his late wife and have it registered on the internet.

Eric did end up naming a star and having it registered on the internet, but he didn't name the star after his late wife. He instead named the star Cliff and he treated it as if it was his friend.

Eric spoke to Cliff every night, even when he wasn't sure if he was really talking to Cliff or whether he'd mistaken Cliff for a different star. Eric had bought a telescope at one point in an effort to see Cliff more clearly, but the telescope wasn't particularly strong and really didn't help very much. The type of telescope Eric would have needed would've cost far more than he was capable of paying. So Eric just did his best to identify Cliff without the aid of an optical instrument and then shared his innermost thoughts with him.

When Eric told Cliff about the compliments class, he knew that if Cliff could speak, he would have told Eric that this was a golden opportunity to meet some good-looking single women.

"You're right, Cliff," said Eric. "I'm going to do it. I'm going to take this compliments class and I'm going to get laid for the first time in a long time."

So Eric signed up for the course, and even though he was quite shy, and even though he was out of practice in the romance department, he knew without a doubt that this class would lead to sex.

As fate would have it, Eric didn't meet a good-looking *single* woman, he met a good-looking *married* woman. Kelly possessed the two qualities Eric was looking for in a partner: she was pretty and she was interested in him.

He fell for her immediately, and he couldn't believe his good fortune when she returned his ardor. This was more than just puppy love. It was "dog love," or whatever was stronger than puppy love. Who knows—it might have even been *wolf* love.

And just a couple days ago he'd finally kissed her lips! And she'd *bit* his! Never before had a woman bit him or scratched him or expressed such passion toward him.

Later that evening, still shaking from the fervor Kelly had stirred in him during their make out session, Eric knew that the next time he found himself with Kelly, he wouldn't be able to contain himself. He'd be forced to rip off her clothes and make passionate love to her, even if it meant taking her to an alley and having sex against a wall like they do in Paris or Lake Tahoe.

And while that would mean that Eric would finally be getting laid for the first time in a long time, it also meant that he would be helping Kelly commit adultery.

Eric then reminded himself that this was a compliments class he was enrolled in, not an adultery class.

At that point, Eric took out a pen and a piece of paper and drafted a letter to Jennifer, his compliments class instructor, and thanked her for everything she'd taught him, and let her know in the nicest way possible that neither she nor any of his fellow students would ever see him again.

21

Steve was a mess the day he met Kelly. His face was battered and bruised from getting his ass kicked by the lumberjacks. It had been a very thorough ass kicking. Several lumberjacks who had been retired for years came back to work just for the day so that they too could get some shots in at Steve.

After the lumberjacks kicked Steve's ass, they went out for a beer to celebrate. Steve was not invited to join them for a beer. Sometimes lumberjacks would invite the guy whose ass they'd kicked to join them for a beer, but not always. In Steve's case, they just left him on the ground.

Steve was getting used to getting his ass kicked recently, so he pulled himself up, even though he was in unspeakable pain. The ribs he thought might have been broken, he now knew were definitely broken thanks to some of the licks the lumberjacks took at them. His right arm was also broken. He knew it was broken because at one point one of the lumberjacks bent Steve's arm and told Steve he was going to break his arm and then he did.

The lumberjack who broke Steve's arm was named Terry. He was one of the retired lumberjacks who came back for the day to help with the ass kicking. He had retired about ten years ago, but when he retired, he told the men they could always call on him if they needed someone's arm broken. He just asked that in return, someone buy him a beer.

Steve could barely breathe; his ass had been kicked so badly. He used his good arm to reach into his wallet to see how much money he had. He had exactly forty dollars. Forty dollars isn't much money these days, and it wasn't much money when Steve was a lumberjack, either. But it was enough to at least get him some food and maybe a cheap motel for a night or two.

Even though they'd broken Steve's ribs and his right arm and punched him in the face and stomach quite a bit, the lumberjacks had shown Steve some mercy in that they didn't take his wallet. Most lumberjack ass kickings included a mugging, but for whatever reason, they didn't mug Steve. Either they let him keep his wallet as a show of respect, or maybe they'd just forgotten to take it. Either way, Steve was glad to at least have a couple bucks on him.

He hobbled out to the road and hitchhiked to the nearest diner.

When the driver dropped Steve off at the diner, Steve asked him if he could give him any money to pay for gas or to help pay to have the bloodstains removed that Steve left on the passenger seat.

"You didn't kill me," said the driver. "That's all I ask of people I pick up. You didn't take my life, so I'm not going to take your money."

Steve thanked the man, walked into the diner, and collapsed into the first booth he saw.

"You're not dying, are you?" said the young waitress who came to take Steve's order.

"I don't think so," said Steve. "Unless there's some internal bleeding going on that I don't know about, I think it's just broken bones."

"Okay," said the waitress. "Our soup today is beef barley. Do you know what you want?"

"Soup sounds good," said Steve. "As I'm talking to you right now, I'm realizing I'm missing a couple of teeth. Probably best not to chew too much."

"Okay," said the waitress, "but if you think you're going to die, let me know so I can call an ambulance. We had a lumberjack die

65

in here a couple months ago. I don't want to have to go through that again."

"That sounds fair," said Steve.

As the waitress set off to get Steve his soup, he caught a glimpse of her name tag. It read KELLY.

Steve couldn't remember the last time he'd had any quality interaction with a woman. It felt good to shoot the breeze with one, even if he was just ordering soup and even if he was currently experiencing more physical pain than he'd ever dreamed possible. He eagerly awaited Kelly's return and tried to think of questions he could ask her.

Kelly started working as a waitress when she was sixteen years old. She was now eighteen and was desperately looking to get out of it. She had a feeling that if she didn't find a new career soon, she would end up waiting tables for the rest of her life.

She'd recently graduated from high school and had no plans to go to college. For whatever reason, she'd always envisioned herself marrying a lumberjack. She wasn't sure if a lumberjack's salary was enough to support two people (and potentially children as well), but she was fairly certain that she would one day wed one, and hopefully she could then give up being a waitress.

The only problem with lumberjacks, Kelly had noticed over the years, was that whenever she met one, they were usually beaten up and bleeding. She thought for sure the guy whose order she'd just taken had to be a lumberjack. He fit the profile.

She had to admit he was kind of cute, too. Kelly currently had a boyfriend who was a freshman in college and was majoring in business, but they rarely saw each other anymore and she knew they couldn't sustain a long distance relationship indefinitely.

Kelly ladled the beef barley into a bowl, grabbed a few packs of crackers, and returned to Steve's booth.

"This look delicious," said Steve as Kelly set the bowl down in front of him.

"Can I ask you a question?" said Kelly.

"Of course," said Steve.

Steve was relieved Kelly had a question for him. He had attempted to come up with some questions to ask her, but in his weakened condition, coupled with his lack of experience talking to members of the opposite sex, he hadn't been able to think of anything to ask her aside from whether or not she liked amusement parks and he wasn't particularly eager to ask her that, so this was an excellent turn of events as Steve saw it.

"Sure," said Steve. "Anything."

"Are you a lumberjack?"

Steve sighed and stared at his beef barley.

"Not anymore," said Steve. "I was. For four days."

Kelly's heart sank and she began to cry, right in front of Steve. She felt silly crying in front of this former lumberjack who had apparently recently been bludgeoned, but for a moment there she thought she had met "the one." She blamed herself for having built things up in her mind so quickly, but there was nothing she could do now other than to let the tears flow. It wasn't a loud, sobbing-type cry she was experiencing, but more of a sniffling, trying-not-to-cry type of cry.

Something about seeing Kelly cry made Steve cry. He wasn't entirely sure why he was crying. Maybe it was because of the physical pain he was experiencing, maybe it was because of the sight of this pretty young lady crying in front of him, or maybe it was because the reality that he could never again work as a lumberjack was finally sinking in.

Steve motioned to Kelly to sit down across from him and they both sat there crying quietly to themselves for a few minutes.

Fortunately for Kelly, it was a slow day at the diner, so no one hounded her for service as she wept.

Eventually, both Steve and Kelly stopped crying and then smiled at each other.

"Well, that was a first," said Steve.

"I'm sorry," said Kelly. "I don't know what happened. That was very unprofessional of me. How's your soup? Did it get cold? I can get you another bowl."

Steve took a sip of the beef barley. "The soup is fine," he said. "But maybe you could get me your phone number?"

Kelly smiled. "Okay."

She took out a pen and wrote her number on a napkin.

"I still live with my mom," she said.

"That's okay," said Steve. "I don't live anywhere."

On the other side of the diner, two men were finishing up their meal and were arguing over which of them was going to pick up the tab.

"I'm paying for this one. You paid for the last one," said one of the men.

"No, *you* paid for the last one. You paid for the last three in fact! I don't need your charity. I'm buying!" said the other man.

Then the first man took a swing at the other man, and just like that, they were in a full-on fight.

Steve, with his background in breaking up fights, reacted the only way he knew how, and that was to get up from his booth and limp over to the two men and stop the fight before either man got seriously hurt.

Kelly watched Steve as he skillfully broke up the fight. He never once raised his voice or touched either man. Up to this point in her young life, she'd never before witnessed someone behave so gracefully in such an intense situation.

She didn't even know this young man's name, but Kelly was fairly certain she would spend the rest of her life with him. She would put her notice in at the diner and they'd run off somewhere and start a new life together. Or maybe they'd just move in with her mother. Before they did anything, though, she knew she'd have to get this battered guy who she'd just shared a cry with to the hospital; his right arm was dangling from his body, leading her to believe it was broken. She was also curious to see what his face looked like under all that blood.

22

"Ta-da!" said Steve. He held up the plastic container to show Kelly he'd eaten the carrot salad.

"What are you doing?" said Kelly. She had just awoken from her drunken slumber and was surprised to see Steve sitting across from her at the table.

"I think the real question is what are *you* doing?" said Steve. "I come home thinking maybe you and I can go out for dinner and a glass of champagne to celebrate, but it looks like you already sucked down an entire winery."

Kelly saw the two empty champagne bottles and realized she must have passed out. Fortunately for Kelly, she was not hungover. People on Kelly's side of the family never got hangovers. Because of that, Kelly's mother had encouraged her to drink from a young age.

"I drank the entire time I was pregnant with you," Kelly remembered her mother telling her. "All my other friends were eating salads and practicing breathing exercises, but I just kept on drinking like I always did, and you turned out great!"

Just like Steve, Kelly's mother was not fond of salads. Kelly never had any luck getting her mom to eat one, so she was quite happy to see that at least her husband had finished his.

"That's great, Steve. It's important we keep the Alzheimer's at bay."

"Yeah," said Steve. "Very important."

Steve waited for Kelly to acknowledge the kitchen was in shambles, but Kelly didn't say anything so Steve decided to force the issue.

"So what's going on here?" said Steve. "Why is there a shredded phone book all over the kitchen? Since when do we even *have* a phone book?"

"We've had a phone book for almost a year!" said Kelly. "It's been on top of the refrigerator! Why don't you pay attention to anything anymore? You're here, but you're not here."

"I'm here but I'm not here?" said Steve. "What the hell is that supposed to mean? All I'm saying is that if there's a phone book in this house, I want to know about it!"

Kelly shook her head and stood up. She took the champagne bottles to the sink, rinsed them, and then started sweeping up the phone book pages that were strewn everywhere.

Steve watched her as she swept and tidied. He didn't offer to help.

"So that's it?" said Steve. "You don't want to talk?"

"Talk about what?" said Kelly.

"I don't know," said Steve, "about you attacking me with a magazine last night, about you locking yourself in the bathroom, about you trashing the kitchen? I mean, take your pick!"

Then Steve pointed to the lipstick on the refrigerator.

"Or how about we talk about how much you like *E*? Maybe that would be a good conversation topic. What's *E*, Kelly? You been doing ecstasy? You got an ecstasy problem? Damnit, Kelly, the last thing I need right now is to have to do a goddamn ecstasy intervention on my wife!"

Kelly had forgotten she'd written *I* ♥ *E* on the refrigerator and ripped up the phone book. She must have done both shortly before passing out, when her mind was at its fuzziest. As she clenched the broom in her hands, she considered answering her husband's question. She also considered smacking him around with the broom. She had to admit it felt good smacking him with a magazine last night. Why stop there?

Eventually Kelly elected to respond to Steve's question with a question of her own:

"What do you want to celebrate?" she said.

"What?" said Steve.

"What do you want to celebrate?" repeated Kelly.

"When I woke up just now, you said you wanted to go out for dinner and a glass of champagne to celebrate. So what are we celebrating?"

Steve found himself at a rare loss for words. Kelly had not been herself the past couple of days. Perhaps this wasn't the best time for him to bring up the Pool Pisser, and how he'd discovered who the culprit was, and how he intended to use their life savings to have this person rubbed out. Perhaps Kelly would not find this whole scenario to be a cause for celebration. Besides, she'd already drunk plenty of champagne. What would be the point of going out now?

And if Steve *did* end up telling Kelly about his plan to eliminate the Pool Pisser, wouldn't that make her an accomplice in the murder, or an accessory, or whatever the term was?

He couldn't believe none of this had occurred to him earlier, but he was glad that it was at least occurring to him now. No, he had to keep as much of this information from his wife as possible. How did he know if he could trust her anyway? Kelly hadn't exactly been a poster child for mental health lately, what with her insistence that Steve eat carrot salads, her beating him with a magazine, her locking herself in the bathroom overnight, and now this trashing of the kitchen.

For the first time, Steve was seeing just how delicate this entire situation was and how important it was for him to choose his words carefully.

Of course, choosing his words carefully had never been one of Steve's strong suits, so instead of responding to his wife's question about what they'd be celebrating in a dignified and measured way, he instead slammed his hand on the refrigerator door as hard as he could and yelled: "WHAT THE FUCK IS *E*?"

23

Chester Rawlings kept a two-liter bottle of hand sanitizer on his desk. That was a fairly large bottle of sanitizer for just one person, but Chester needed a large bottle, as he applied sanitizer to his hands after each of his smoke breaks. He also kept several tins of breath mints on hand at all times, and when he thought to purchase them, packs of chewing gum as well.

Chester appreciated that in this day and age his coworkers at the gym and the gym members didn't give him a hard time about smoking in public, and in an effort to repay their benevolence, he figured the least he could do was sufficiently mask the smell of the cigarettes at the conclusion of each smoking session.

He'd popped two pieces of wintergreen-flavored gum in his mouth and was in the process of applying sanitizer to his hands when two men dressed in black appeared in his doorway.

"Good morning, gentlemen," said Chester. "Can I help you?"

"Are you the manager?" said the first man.

"Yes," said Chester.

"Chester Rawlings?" said the second man.

"That's right."

He didn't officially invite the men into his office, but that didn't stop them from walking in and sitting down in the two chairs across from Chester's desk.

Chester took a look at the men. They were both stocky and both had facial hair. One of the men had a goatee and the other man seemed to be on the verge of growing a goatee. Their graying hair was slicked back and tied in little ponytails. Chester figured the two men were brothers as they were strikingly similar in appearance.

"You're a smoker, huh?" said the first man, sniffing the air. "I smell smoke."

Chester smiled. "Afraid I am."

"Kinda funny, isn't it?" said the second man. "A manager of a gym who smokes."

"Not a habit I'm proud of," said Chester. "I smoke three to five cigarettes a day at work. I smoke more when I'm at home. But when I'm at work, I try to limit it to three to five."

"Sends a strange message, though," said the first man. "A manager of a gym who smokes."

Chester leaned back in his chair and clasped his hands over his stomach. These men sure were interested in his smoking habits.

"You guys sure are interested in my smoking habits," said Chester. "There's a liquor store down the street if you're looking to buy some cigarettes. I'm afraid we don't sell them here. Just gym memberships."

"I think you misunderstood us," said the second man. "That's what we're here for. Gym memberships."

In Chester's experience, when people came to the gym to buy memberships, they usually told him that right off the bat. They didn't ask him questions about his smoking and they didn't just invite themselves into his office without him first asking them to come in and have a seat.

He wondered if having these two men as members would enhance the gym's character or if it would detract from it. That was one of the things he had to consider when reviewing gym applications. It was a privilege to be a member of a gym, after all, not a right. And for whatever reason, Chester was suspicious of these two men. They didn't give off that air of open-mindedness that was crucial for all gym members to possess if a gym was going to function at a high level.

But perhaps he was judging these men prematurely. They'd only been in his presence for a couple of minutes, and maybe under their gruff exteriors were engaging, agreeable gym members just waiting to get out.

Chester hoped that was indeed the case as he handed each man a clipboard with the requisite papers.

The first man flipped through the pages. "Jesus Christ, you'd think we were a couple of Mexicans applying for temporary work Visas. You want a blood test, too?"

"It doesn't take as long to fill out as you'd think," said Chester as pleasantly as possible. "Just let me know if you have any questions."

The second man pulled out a pair of reading glasses and put them on. "Vision isn't what it used to be," he smiled, "but I'm fifty-two now. What're you gonna do?"

Chester beamed. "Well how about that? You say you're fifty-two? That happens to be my exact age."

"No shit," said the second man.

"No shit," said Chester.

Then all three men shared a smile, sitting there in mutual admiration. Chester made it a point to smile several times a day, so this wasn't anything new to him, but for the two men, genuine smiles had always been hard to come by. There just wasn't a lot of smiling done in their line of work.

Yet here they were, sitting in Chester's office, applying for gym memberships they didn't even want, and smiling from ear to ear.

"Gum?" said Chester, offering the pack of wintergreen-flavored chewing gum.

Both men took a piece and chewed their gum as they filled out their gym applications to the best of their abilities, occasionally asking Chester for guidance whenever they got hung up on a question.

24

Steve and Kelly were married in Las Vegas, only eight days after they'd met at the diner. They went to a small chapel and requested to be married by an Elvis impersonator. They were told that the Elvis impersonator was sick, but they could instead be married by a Little Richard impersonator or a David Lee Roth impersonator.

Since there was of course no shortage of Elvis impersonators in Vegas, Steve and Kelly briefly considered going to another chapel so they could be married by "The King." However, they had to admit that neither of them were particularly big Elvis fans, so why hassle going to another chapel when they were already at this one?

They were ultimately wed by the David Lee Roth impersonator, as his rate was the most economically convenient.

After they'd formed their union, Steve and Kelly moved in with Kelly's mother. Steve had no job, and was still recovering from getting his ass kicked by the lumberjacks. Kelly continued working at the diner and while she was at work, Steve and Kelly's mother would sit in the living room, watch TV, and drink.

Kelly's mother was named Tammy and she wasn't particularly pretty.

Under different circumstances, Tammy might have been prettier, but she drank a lot and she didn't exercise or watch what she ate, and overall she had a bit of a defeatist attitude, and because of that she looked maybe fifteen years older than she actually was. This was at a time when eating right and exercising and thinking positively weren't yet in vogue, and because of that, people's appearances occasionally suffered.

However, there was a time when Tammy was much prettier, and during that time she interned at the local news station. At that time, internships were in their infancy; most people didn't even know what an internship was. In fact, Tammy didn't really know what an internship was either when she applied for the internship at the local news station.

She had seen the flyer advertising the internship in the hallway of one of the buildings at the community college where she was taking a typing class and she thought that it sounded like an interesting opportunity, whatever it was.

So she went to the news station and told them she wanted to intern for them and they told her they would consider her, but only if no one else applied. A week went by and no one else applied and the news station got sick of waiting for other applicants so they hired Tammy to be their very first intern.

The news station didn't really know what interning entailed, either, but they'd heard somewhere that it was a good way to get young people to work for you without having to pay them anything, so they thought they'd give it a try.

Tammy reported to the weatherman. Her duties, among other things, included getting him coffee, answering his phone, obtaining snacks for him when he was hungry, and making sure he had whatever information he needed for that night's telecast to ensure that he gave the most accurate weather report possible.

Sleeping with the weatherman was not one of her required tasks, but she did that too. Tammy and the weatherman slept together fairly frequently and eventually Tammy became pregnant with Kelly.

Once Tammy knew for sure that she was pregnant, she informed the weatherman. The weatherman asked Tammy if it was possible that he was not actually the father. Tammy told the weatherman that he was the only person she'd slept with in recent memory and the only other times she'd slept with anyone was in high school (which had been a few years ago at that point), so clearly none of those encounters way back then could have led to her current pregnancy.

Tammy was not in love with the weatherman and the weatherman was not in love with Tammy. But the weatherman had a fair amount of money and he told Tammy he would give her whatever amount of money she wanted, just as long as she never told anyone that he was the father of her child.

So Tammy accepted an undisclosed amount of money from the weatherman and used it to raise Kelly. The payment wasn't so big that Tammy didn't ever have to work again, so after Tammy ended her internship at the news station, she ended up working at a grocery store for many years. But thanks to the payment from the weatherman, she was never short of money.

Tammy took great pride in keeping her word, so she never let anyone know that the weatherman was Kelly's father. She assumed that confidentiality extended to her daughter as well, so when Kelly grew to an age where she naturally started asking questions about her father's identity, Tammy would simply tell her she didn't know who he was.

"I don't know who your father is," Tammy would say. "That happens sometimes. Sometimes people don't know who their fathers are."

One might think that Kelly would have pressed her mother harder to obtain further information about her father, but Kelly just never made it a priority. She knew her mother loved her and her mother always took excellent care of her, and besides, most of her friends who had fathers would tell Kelly how their fathers bossed them around all the time and gave them curfews and wouldn't let them drink and didn't hug them enough, and as far as they were concerned, Kelly was fortunate to *not* have a father. She could do whatever she wanted!

Steve and Tammy now found themselves sitting in the living room of Tammy's house while Kelly was at work. They were drinking and watching TV. Tammy was on her ninth or tenth drink. Tammy never got hangovers (no one on her side of the family ever did), so it was okay for her to drink as much as she wanted. Steve was on his third drink. He was drinking whiskey, neat. Tammy drank mostly gin and tonics.

The show on TV was pretty boring, so Steve decided to ask Tammy about her husband, since he never seemed to be around.

"I never married," said Tammy.

"Oh," said Steve.

Tammy didn't say anything else and Steve wasn't sure if he should ask any follow-up questions because Kelly had mentioned while she and Steve were driving to Vegas that she didn't know who her father was and when Steve had told her that he found that to be unusual, she'd shrugged and asked if they could talk about something else.

So it probably wasn't polite for Steve to ask Tammy who Kelly's father was, but the TV show was pretty boring and Steve was on his third drink and there was a lull in the conversation, so Steve said, "This is probably none of my business, but Kelly told me she doesn't know who her father is."

"None of us do," said Tammy.

This would have been a nice opportunity for Tammy to ask Steve about his parents, in an effort to deflect the topic of conversation away from the identity of Kelly's father, but Tammy was no stranger to hiding the identity of Kelly's father, and she'd learned over the years that whenever anyone started asking questions about him, it was best for her to give terse answers and then just sit in silence until the interested parties changed the subject themselves.

So Tammy and Steve sat in silence for a little while, but the TV show was so unbelievably boring and there were no other channels to choose from, and the third whiskey was making Steve feel incredibly chatty, so he started talking about his parents, even though it was not one of his favorite topics. He figured his new mother-in-law would ask about them at some point anyway, so why not talk about them now?

"I know who my father is," said Steve, "but we don't talk much. Actually, we don't talk at all. But I write him letters now and then to let him know how I am."

"I think that's wonderful you at least write to him," said Tammy.

"Yeah. I don't know much about my mother. She died when I was two or three years old."

"I'm sorry to hear that."

"She wouldn't allow anyone to take pictures of her, but I have this." Steve reached into his wallet and pulled out a small, somewhat tattered picture of the tree from his backyard. He handed it to Tammy.

"Is this an oak tree?" said Tammy.

"Yes," said Steve.

"It's beautiful," said Tammy.

25

Steve had the baleen whale dream again. Usually when he had the baleen whale dream, the dream would start out with Steve in human form, and then he'd transform into a baleen whale. But this time around, he was a baleen whale the entire time.

He was swimming in the ocean and he was craving ketchup. No matter where he looked, though, there was no ketchup to be found.

He kept swimming and swimming, and eventually he came across a giant crate that was slowly sinking to the bottom of the ocean. Baleen whales most likely cannot read in real life, but since this was a dream, Steve was able to read the word KETCHUP that was printed in large letters on the side of the crate.

Steve swam toward the crate, but the crate started to sink faster and faster, and no matter how fast Steve swam, he could not catch the crate. It just sank deeper and deeper toward the bottom of the ocean.

As Steve continued to chase after the crate of ketchup and continued to swim toward the bottom of the ocean, he was almost positive he could make out a shopping mall—but who would build a shopping mall at the bottom of the ocean?

Steve's final thought before waking up was that if there indeed was a shopping mall at the bottom of the ocean, not many people would visit it, so at least there would be no shortage of places to park.

"Coffee?" said Kelly.

Kelly was standing in the kitchen brewing coffee. Steve was sitting at the kitchen table; he was beginning to realize he'd slept there all night.

Last night, when Steve and Kelly were having their argument and Steve wasn't telling Kelly what he wanted to celebrate and Kelly wasn't telling Steve what E was, Steve had told Kelly that he was going to sit at the table and he wasn't going to move until Kelly fessed up. Kelly told Steve that was fine with her and she went upstairs and slept in their bed.

Steve rubbed his eyes and yawned. "I had the whale dream again."

Kelly sat down at the table and put a cup of coffee in front of Steve. He hadn't answered her question as to whether he wanted coffee or not, but it didn't bother her all that much, as she'd grown accustomed to him not listening to her.

"I think I'm having an affair," said Kelly.

Steve might not have been a good listener, but he definitely heard *that*.

"WHAT?"

"I think I'm having an affair," said Kelly. "His name is Eric. That's what E is."

Steve took a sip of his coffee and burned the roof of his mouth. It always pissed him off when he did that, and he did it a lot. He'd been drinking hot beverages his entire life, but he always forgot exactly how hot they were until it was too late. He also realized that he really needed to urinate, but at the same time, he felt frozen in his chair. He couldn't go to the bathroom at a time like this, not after his wife just dropped that bombshell on him.

"Well," said Steve, "are you having an affair or not? What do you mean you *think* you're having an affair?"

"I'm not going to get into that right now," said Kelly. "You probably wouldn't listen to me anyway. I don't feel like classifying it as anything at the moment, although I'm fairly certain that whatever it is, it's trending in the direction of an affair."

Kelly held her hands around her coffee mug. She loved the sensation of a cup of coffee warming her hands. Truth be told, she liked holding coffee more than she liked drinking it. The holding part was like a form of meditation for her.

"Now," said Kelly, "I've answered your question. Now I want you to answer mine. What exactly did you want to celebrate?"

Steve was definitely taken aback to learn that his wife may or may not be cheating on him. But then he thought about how over the years he'd asked women if they were single and how even though he didn't consider that question to be a pickup line, he had to admit to himself that by asking random women that question, maybe he hadn't been entirely faithful to Kelly. And maybe in some way, his actions had led to the possibility of this type of situation arising.

Then again, he'd been providing for his wife for a long time and where did she get off running around maybe having affairs with guys named Eric? Steve was the one (at least until recently) who was going to work every day and bringing home the bacon, and hell, she couldn't even let him have his Pizza Munch Wednesdays without making a big stink about how he wasn't paying enough attention to her and then she's trying to make him eat salads, and damnit, that's why he was going to the gym! He was going to the gym and working out so he could eat as much Pizza Munch as he damn well wanted without gaining any weight and so he wouldn't have to eat salads and now he couldn't even go in the pool anymore because of some pissing desperado who thought he could take a leak anywhere he damn well pleased and at any rate it was too early in the morning for this and Steve was so damn tired and his wife was no longer being faithful to him and so he just came clean.

"There's a guy pissing in the pool at the gym, and it's been bothering me for a long time, and I found out who he was and I arranged for a couple of guys to kill him and that's what I wanted to celebrate."

For a second, Kelly thought maybe her husband was joking. She *hoped* he was joking. But then it quickly dawned on her that Steve didn't have much in the way of a sense of humor anymore, and that he most definitely wasn't joking.

Kelly took a deep breath. "Did I hear you correctly? Did you just say you're arranging to have someone *murdered?*"

"I knew you wouldn't understand," said Steve. "And not only do you not understand, but now I've implicated you through no fault of my own. You have unwittingly become an accomplice and an accessory. I wish you hadn't pushed me so hard. I was trying to keep this from you for your own protection."

"I don't think your legal jargon, or whatever it is you're trying to say, is a hundred percent accurate," said Kelly. "But, Steve! *Murder? Seriously?* What is wrong with you? WHAT THE HELL IS WRONG WITH YOU?"

"What's *wrong* with me?" yelled Steve. "I'll tell you what's wrong with me! My dad never gave me a fucking chance in life! That's what's wrong with me. You know he never let me wear a baseball glove when I played little league and you know that prick never let me eat at diners and you know he never told me a fucking thing about my mother, except that she was a 'wonderful woman!' I basically had to raise myself! You think I wanted to become a lumberjack because I was *happy?* You know all the sick things that demented son of a bitch did to me and yet you still ask me what's *wrong* with me? I think what we should be focusing on is what's wrong with *you!* You're the one getting drunk and writing lovey-dovey messages to your boy toy on our refrigerator!"

Kelly thought to herself that this must be what the end of a marriage felt like. She was now most likely cheating on her husband while her husband was spending his days plotting to kill someone. If this wasn't a classic example of a marriage hitting rock bottom, then what exactly was it?

It was such a shame, too. They were coming up on their thirtieth wedding anniversary. Sure, things hadn't been going well between them for a while now, but sometimes a milestone anniversary was all it took to put a rocky marriage back on track. Sadly, they would never have an opportunity to know for sure, because Kelly had no desire to be married to Steve for one second longer. There was simply no way she could live under the same roof as an aspiring killer.

Kelly wasn't saying anything, and that was making Steve very nervous. She was clearly very upset with him. Again. She was always getting upset with him these days. What was she going to do? Was she going to lock herself in the bathroom again? Was she going to leave him? Was she going to report him to the authorities?

And Steve hadn't even told Kelly that he'd planned on using their life savings to have the Pool Pisser eliminated. And he hadn't told her that he'd been unemployed for over a month, and he hadn't told her that he hadn't actually eaten the carrot salad. What if she found out about *those* things? Then she'd really blow her stack.

Damnit! Why did he have to have the whale dream again? Waking up from that dream always got his day off on the wrong foot. And why had Kelly confronted him about all these things immediately after he'd woken up? He was groggy and his defenses were down. He knew better than to confess to her about the impending murder, a murder that with any luck was taking place right now. But the cat was out of the bag and whether or not he would ultimately get away with the murder was now basically in the hands of his very angry wife. He'd only been awake for a few minutes, but this was already shaping up to be the worst day of Steve's life.

"What are you thinking?" said Steve.

Kelly was staring into her coffee mug. She didn't look up. "I'm thinking that in this moment I can't think of a single compliment to give you."

She let those words linger for a moment as she took a sip of her coffee. Then she said, "You know I could have married a business major?"

"What?" said Steve.

"When you and I met. When I was working at that horrible diner. I never told you, but I was dating a business major. His name was Michael and we were in love. But in the back of my mind, I always wanted to marry a lumberjack. Then you walked in, and you were all beat up, and you were so helpless, but you somehow found the strength to break up that fight. And even though you were no longer a lumberjack at that point and had no hope of becoming a lumberjack again, I knew you were the one for me. And now... here we are."

Kelly became silent again. Steve wished his wife would beat him with a magazine, or rip up the phone book some more, or pester him about his Pizza Munch Wednesdays. But it was clear she wasn't going to do any of those things. It was clear she was going to be silent, and it was the kind of silence that Steve recognized as very bad silence.

Kelly stood up and began walking down the hallway.

"Babe!" said Steve, trailing Kelly down the hallway. "Babe! I can explain!"

Just then, there was a knock at the front door. Kelly was planning to go upstairs and pack some things and then drive somewhere. She wasn't concerned with where she drove exactly, just as long as it was far away from her husband.

Since she was the one closest to the door, she opened it. She expected it to maybe be someone from the gas company or maybe an upbeat young adult wanting her to sign some type of petition, but when she opened the door she instead found a neatly dressed older gentleman with silver hair and a mustache. He wore glasses and was holding a wooden boat in each hand.

"Hi," said the man. "You must be Kelly. I've heard a lot about you. My name's Jerry. I'm Steve's father."

26

Chester Rawlings was giving the two men a tour of the gym. He and the men were all still chewing their bubble gum.

It was fortunate for Chester that he was meeting the two men now, because if he had met them at another time, he would already be dead.

That's how the two men had always operated. Someone would tell them that they wanted someone killed, and they would give the men some money, and then the men would kill the specified person. They wouldn't hang out with the person they were supposed to kill. They wouldn't get to know them. They'd simply kill them and then be on their way.

But the two men were at a point in their careers where they were openly questioning whether or not they needed to continue killing people. Sure, they enjoyed the work. They were good at it; it gave them a sense of purpose, and the money was fantastic.

The problem was they couldn't think of what they'd do with their lives if they *didn't* kill people. They weren't going to sit around watching TV all day; they didn't like TV. They weren't going to take up golf. They had no desire to travel, and while at one point the two men had discussed opening a horse ranch that would also offer hot air balloon rides, the likelihood of that happening anytime soon seemed marginal at best.

The two men had got their start in the killing business the way most people did, by killing a carnival worker when they were kids.

It had been one of those midway games where you needed to throw a softball into a large milk can with a very small opening, and if you succeeded, you were rewarded with a giant stuffed animal of your choice.

The two men were two boys at that point. One of them was twelve and the other was ten. Even at such young ages, they knew the odds of winning those types of games were not in their favor, and required more luck than actual skill.

In other words, they knew better than to spend all their lawn-mowing money on a rigged carnival game in order to win a stuffed animal that they could certainly live without.

The carnival worker should have known better than to have laughed at them as ball after ball clanged off the tops of the milk cans. The carnival worker didn't really care whether they won or not, but he was a carnival worker, and he knew it was expected of him to be annoying and make fun of the people playing his game.

The boys didn't know that was how it was supposed to work, though. All they knew was that they'd lost fourteen dollars, plus the carny had teased them mercilessly, so they decided he would have to pay for what he'd done.

Their father didn't own guns, but there were hammers in the house. So both boys took a hammer from their father's shop and then went back to the carnival to wait for it to close.

The carny didn't see them as he was closing down his stand. It was unfortunate that this particular carny took so long to close down his stand because all the other carnies had already closed down their stands and gone home, so they weren't there to witness the two boys sneak up on him and bludgeon him repeatedly with their hammers.

There wasn't much of a police investigation done when the carnival worker was found dead the next morning. It was one of those situations where there wasn't exactly a public outcry, because most people throughout history have found carnival workers to be fairly irritating. Plus, carnival workers knew that in their line of work there was a high death rate and they simply accepted the fact they were taking their lives into their own hands whenever they reported for duty.

So when the body was discovered, the other carnival workers said a silent prayer to themselves, thanked God it hadn't been them, and then went back to harassing the people who were wasting their money playing their games.

That was a long time ago, and the two men hadn't stopped killing since.

"Here's the pool," said Chester as he led the two men into the gym's aquatic center.

A young man swimming laps noticed Chester. He stopped, lifted his swimming goggles, and rested them on his head.

"Hey, Chester!" he said. "Race ya?"

Chester waved to the young man. "No, sir. Just ate!" He patted his stomach and pretended to be full.

"Yeah, right!" said the young man. He smiled, put his goggles back on, and continued his laps.

"You swim?" said the first man.

"Not anymore," said Chester. "But before I started smoking, I was a competitive swimmer."

"No shit," said the second man.

"No shit," said Chester.

The first man took a long look at the pool and then said to Chester, "Let me ask you something. Hypothetically speaking, do people piss in this thing?"

Chester let out a chuckle. "That's been a popular question lately."

"Hypothetically speaking," said the second man, "if someone was whizzing in the pool, would you be able to track it?"

"Track it?" said Chester. "No. But I guarantee you there is no more urine in this pool than you'd find in any other pool in the country. Our pool's pH and chlorine levels are checked daily and we scored a ninety-eight on our most recent inspection. This pool is as clean as it gets."

The two men mulled over what Chester had just told them. His story seemed to check out. There were currently a dozen or so people in the pool and everyone looked happy.

Even if they were swimming in a cesspool of urine, no one appeared to be getting hurt. They couldn't leave without asking one more question, though, and the man who appeared to be on the verge of growing a goatee asked it:

"You ever pee in the pool?"

Chester laughed again. That was one of the things that had endeared him to the gym members over the years: his humor. He was always willing to answer all gym members' questions patiently, and always with a smile on his face. There was never a question that was too absurd or challenging for Chester to respond to without grace.

In fact, the only time Chester had ever lost his cool with a gym member was when Steve kept badgering him about someone pissing in the pool. But when Chester lost his cool then, it wasn't as a gym manager. He lost his cool as a friend feeling betrayed by another friend. Well, maybe *betrayed* was a bit harsh, but Steve did play the same-age card on Chester and Chester had no patience for that kind of behavior and that's why he had to set a boundary with Steve.

Now these two men were standing in front of him, asking him similar questions to the ones Steve had raised regarding the pool's urine levels, albeit in a far less accusatory tone. Maybe these two men were here for a reason. Maybe they were here to give Chester a second chance to discuss this topic and to give him the opportunity this time around to keep his composure. And even though this question the man on the verge of growing a goatee had just asked was of a very personal nature, Chester nonetheless elected to answer it honestly.

"You bet I have," said Chester. "I've peed in pools all over the world. When you're a competitive swimmer, sometimes you don't have a choice. You're in the water for long periods at a stretch, and sometimes there isn't time for a bathroom break. So you just go. Sometimes I'd even go while in the middle of a race."

"So you've whizzed in this pool," said the first man.

"This pool?" said Chester. "No. I've never even been in this pool. Haven't been in the water in eleven years. And even if I was still swimming competitively, I definitely wouldn't urinate in this pool. I'm the gym's manager. What kind of message would that send if I was going to the bathroom in the very pool that I manage? My freewheeling days as a competitive swimmer and pissing wherever and whenever I want are long gone."

The two men nodded to each other and both appeared to be thinking the same thing: Chester was clean.

"So, gentlemen," said Chester, "unless you have any further questions, would you like to make this official? Joining a gym can be one of the greatest gifts you can give your body."

The men had almost forgotten they'd filled out those applications.

"We need to think about it some more," said the first man.

"Take all the time you like," said Chester, "and I'll do this for you—if you sign a one-year contract today, I'll give you ten percent off."

Chester pulled his cigarettes out of his pocket. "Now if you'll excuse me, I'm going to step outside for a smoke."

The second man, the one who was fifty-two and who appeared to be on the verge of growing a goatee, felt a tinge of sadness. He wasn't used to getting to know the people he was supposed to kill and he was really enjoying the conversation he and his brother were having with Chester. He wasn't quite ready for it to end.

"We'll join you," he said.

27

Steve and Kelly lived with Tammy for about two months. It was around that time that Steve healed up and felt well enough to work again. Kelly was excited for Steve to start working because she was ready to retire from the waitressing business.

It was also around that time that Kelly and Tammy had a big argument. Their argument, more than Steve feeling better, might have been the real catalyst that led to Steve and Kelly moving out.

The argument was over salads. Kelly had a night off from work and decided to cook for Steve and Tammy. She had wanted Tammy to eat more salads because she knew if her mother took better care of her body that her mother would be prettier than she currently was and Kelly knew Tammy was capable of looking a lot prettier than she did.

So Kelly served Tammy and Steve big salads as an appetizer for their dinner. Tammy told Kelly that she was going to skip the salad and drink another gin and tonic instead.

Steve was still a good husband to Kelly at that point in their marriage, so even though he wasn't a fan of salads, he still had a few bites to show Kelly his appreciation for her cooking.

Kelly was used to her mother not eating salads, and while she didn't really expect her to eat the salad she'd prepared for her, it was still pissing her off quite a bit that she'd dismissed it so quickly, so Kelly decided to start an argument.

"How many gin and tonics have you had today?"

"I've had seven. Maybe eight. And two Mai Tais."

"And do you really think it's good to drink that much?"

Tammy was used to her daughter periodically questioning her about her alcohol consumption, so she didn't feel especially threatened by Kelly's pointed question.

"I can drink as much as I want," said Tammy. "I don't get hangovers. And neither do you. No one in our family does. So would you like me to make you a gin and tonic, too?"

Kelly was really in a foul mood. The night before at the diner she waited on a fussy man who sent his eggs back *five* times. She had never served a customer who'd been that particular about his food before.

And even though Kelly made sure the cook spit in the eggs and put a few hairs in them each time the customer demanded a fresh order, it still didn't give her any gratification. She really wanted to sock the guy in the throat.

Then to top it all off, the customer didn't give Kelly a tip and he said that she and the diner were lucky that he was paying them anything at all since he'd just had the worst dining experience "in the history of the world."

Maybe Kelly had to take that kind of abuse from a paying customer at her job, but she didn't have to take that kind of abuse from her mother—her mother who drank the entire time she'd been pregnant with Kelly, who never told Kelly who her father was, and who rarely complimented Kelly on anything.

"No, I don't want a gin and tonic," said Kelly. "I want a salad. Just because people on our side of the family can drink as much as they want without getting hangovers doesn't mean we *should* drink as much as we want."

"Well, all I know," said Tammy, "is that I'm a grown woman and I can make my own choices, and this is my house and I don't have to eat salads in my own house if I don't want to, and if you don't like it, you can move out!"

Then Kelly told Tammy that she and Steve were already more or less planning on moving out since Steve was feeling better, and then Kelly accused Tammy of not giving her enough compliments and not being particularly supportive of her over the years and then Tammy fired back that she'd provided food and shelter for Kelly her entire life and how dare she suggest that Tammy wasn't a supportive mother, and in her anger Tammy blurted out that she sort of had a dream to work at a news station at one point in her life and she interned at a news station in pursuit of that dream, but then she had to give up the dream and go work at a grocery store so she could raise Kelly.

Steve sat there frozen as the two women went back and forth. Steve was trained in breaking up physical fights, but he had no idea how to break up arguments—especially mother-daughter arguments. So he just did his best to stay out of the line of fire.

As it turned out, Steve didn't have to do anything anyway, because it was that last thing that Tammy told Kelly—the thing about how she'd interned at a news station—that gave Kelly pause.

"Wait a minute," said Kelly, "did you say you interned at a news station?"

It was now dawning on Tammy as she worked on her ninth gin and tonic of the day that she'd never told Kelly about her internship at the news station.

"Well… yes," said Tammy.

Kelly was confused. "Did they even have internships back then?"

"Yes," said Tammy. "But they were still relatively new and intern responsibilities weren't clearly defined, and as a result a lot of people got hurt."

A light bulb went off in Kelly's head. Sure, she hadn't badgered her mother much over the years for information about her father (Kelly's friends had always told her that she was better off without one and she'd always taken her friends' word on the matter), but now Kelly had her mother on the ropes and this time around she wasn't about to let her off the hook.

"So my father worked at the news station, right?"

"I can't confirm or deny that."

Kelly smirked. "Why else would you give up a news station internship to go work at a grocery store? You couldn't be pregnant *and* intern at the news station? I don't understand."

Tammy took a long, slow pull from her gin and tonic. She wanted to tell her daughter about her father. She really did. But she had made a promise to him that she would never reveal his identity. And as much as Tammy dreaded eating salads, she dreaded the idea of talking to her daughter about who her father was even more.

Yes, many years had passed since she'd had the affair with the weatherman, but if Kelly found out about it, she would no doubt attempt to contact the weatherman, and if the weatherman still had the same wife, and if his wife caught wind of it, she would no doubt fly off the handle and accuse Tammy of being a homewrecker, and Tammy had avoided being labeled a homewrecker for over nineteen years—a streak she was not about to give up without a fight.

But instead of fighting, Tammy took a whiff of the salad that was still sitting in front of her and said, "You know, this salad *does* look delicious. I think I'll give it a try after all."

Kelly didn't say anything to her mother after her mother told her that her salad looked delicious. Kelly wouldn't take her compliments class until many years later, but even without the benefit of professional training, she still knew what a backhanded compliment sounded like, and she wasn't about to dignify Tammy's backhanded compliment with any kind of response. Instead, she stood up from the table, went up to her room, and started packing.

The next morning, Steve and Kelly were sitting in Kelly's car in front of Tammy's house. They'd packed their things and were ready to start their new life, even if they didn't know exactly where they were going or what they would be doing. Kelly considered calling the diner to let them know she wouldn't be working there anymore. She ultimately decided against it and figured if she just stopped showing up, they'd eventually get the idea.

Kelly didn't say goodbye to Tammy. Steve attempted to calm Kelly down and tried to explain to her that her mother was not a jerk.

"It's not like she's a pharmacist," said Steve. "She's actually a pretty nice person. And I know you said she doesn't give out compliments very easily, but the other night I showed her the picture of my mom and she said it was 'beautiful.'"

"That doesn't count," said Kelly. "She loves trees. Always has. It's no accomplishment to get her to say something positive about a tree."

Steve realized he wasn't going to get anywhere with Kelly—she was still too upset with her mother. She was even too upset to properly quit her job. He decided to drop it. Besides, who was he to judge? He'd run away from his father, so why couldn't Kelly run away from her mother?

"I'm thinking we should go east," said Steve.

"That sounds good," said Kelly.

"I'm not worried about finding work," said Steve. "There's secret lumberjack societies in every town. I'll just tell them I used to be a lumberjack and they'll point me in the right direction for a job."

Kelly frowned. "But Steve, didn't lumberjacks beat you within an inch of your life? Do you really think they have your best interests in mind?"

"It's a society for *former* lumberjacks," said Steve. "If it was active lumberjacks, yeah, they'd probably put me through a wall. But no one in these organizations is a current lumberjack, which means they've all gotten their asses kicked severely at one time or another like I did. I overheard guys talk about these groups when I was still in the business, and they'll help us out."

Kelly smiled and leaned over to give Steve a kiss.

Steve turned the ignition and looked back at the house to see if Tammy was watching them from a window. She wasn't.

As he pulled away from the curb, Steve thought about how he'd miss the evenings he spent drinking and watching TV with Tammy.

However, he definitely wouldn't miss the hangovers.

28

Eric was sitting in his car across the street from Steve and Kelly's house. He'd slept in his car overnight. He hadn't intended to sleep there, but that's what ended up happening.

Ever since Eric dropped the compliments class, he couldn't stop thinking about Kelly. By quitting the class, he was attempting to take the high road. He knew if he continued to attend the course, his hunger for Kelly would have continued to grow until he had no choice left but to passionately remove every article of her clothing and have sex with her against a wall.

And while the thought of having wall sex with Kelly appealed to Eric a great deal, he couldn't look past the fact that Kelly was married, and any kind of sex with her—wall sex or otherwise— simply could not occur.

Eric was shocked that his star, Cliff, didn't see it the same way. According to Cliff, if two consenting adults wanted to engage in hot sex that was up to them, and they did not need to first receive permission from a spouse just because one of them happened to be married.

"Are you sure about that, Cliff? I thought marriage vows ran a lot deeper than that. Why would you make vows in the first place if you didn't plan on keeping them?"

Cliff didn't answer Eric, of course, because Cliff was a star and couldn't talk. But Eric could *feel* Cliff's messages and the message Eric received from Cliff was that he needed to get in his car and drive to Kelly's house and have sex with her.

Cliff also let it be known that he was not thrilled with Eric's decision to quit the compliments class without first consulting him. He let Eric know that a lot of the inner turmoil he was experiencing could have been avoided entirely if he'd simply stayed the course and pursued his feelings for Kelly instead of attempting to suppress them.

So Eric went into his house, pulled out his phone book, and located Kelly's address. He psyched himself up and then got in his Saturn and drove to her home. It had been a few days since he'd last seen her and he knew she would be upset with him for dropping the class abruptly, but he would explain to her the strong "wolf love" feelings he'd been experiencing and that although he didn't want to help her commit adultery, he....

He didn't know what he'd say, exactly. But the important thing was that he was going to say *something*.

Eric was scared shitless when he pulled up to Kelly's house. As soon as he put the Saturn in park and killed the ignition, he knew he had to get out of the car immediately. If he sat there for any time at all, his mind would go to work on him and he'd start playing all kinds of scenarios over and over in his head, and then he'd lose any momentum he'd built up in terms of confronting Kelly and then he wouldn't get out of the car at all, and then he'd drive home and boy would Cliff be disappointed when he broke the news to him that he'd driven all the way to Kelly's only to do nothing but turn around and drive home again.

So Eric immediately opened the driver's side door and readied himself to ring Kelly's bell in hopefully more ways than one. He didn't know if her husband was home and frankly, he didn't care. This was *wolf love*, goddamnit, and wolf love had a momentum of its own that could not be stopped by anything.

As Eric started to cross the street to Kelly's house, a white car came darting around the corner and pulled into her driveway. Eric watched a stocky man get out of the car and go into the house.

Eric figured the man had to be Kelly's husband. And even though Eric had just worked himself up to confront Kelly, no matter the circumstances, and confess his undying love for her, he started to have second thoughts. At least, he knew he definitely didn't want to share his powerful feelings with her if her husband was home. And what if Kelly wasn't even home herself?

Eric was in his head now. He started to imagine all the different scenarios that could play out if he chose to ring Kelly's doorbell, and none of the scenarios ended well for him.

He stood there and thought about how love—any love—(even wolf love!) had its limits and could only carry a man so far, and that ultimately all love, regardless of the momentum it possessed, could eventually be stamped out.

Thinking those thoughts made Eric very sad. He got back in his car, but didn't drive anywhere. He just sat there and sulked. About an hour later, he fell asleep.

29

"These are absolutely darling," said Kelly.

She was sitting at the kitchen table with Steve's father, enjoying the two little wooden boats he'd brought.

One of the boats was dolphin blue and had STEVE painted on it. The other boat was amaranth purple and had KELLY painted on it. Both boats had eyes and mouths painted on them to give them a human feel, and Kelly's boat had lush eyelashes drawn around the eyes.

Even amid the chaos of the morning, with her getting into what was most likely a marriage-ending argument with her husband and then meeting her father-in-law for the very first time only moments later, Kelly was still able to make a mental note that she'd just paid Steve's father a compliment, and therefore only had nine people to go to reach her required quota of complimenting ten different people every day.

Kelly thought to herself that no matter what kind of chaos Steve might bring into their lives, she would stay disciplined and make her compliments quota every single day, come hell or high water.

Steve elected not to sit at the kitchen table with Kelly and his father. He instead locked himself in the guest bathroom in the hallway.

Steve hadn't seen his father in person since he was eighteen, but he was in no mood to catch up and reminisce, what with his marriage most likely falling apart, not to mention the whole murder thing he was attempting to pull off. Those were not the types of things anyone would be eager to share with an estranged parent right off the bat.

So instead of saying hello to his father when he saw him standing there in his doorway, Steve simply muttered, "For the love of fuck," and then let himself into the hallway bathroom and shut the door behind him.

Fortunately for Steve, his beloved bottle of cologne was in his bag near the front door, so he was able to grab it before locking himself in the bathroom. His father—who Steve loathed and wanted absolutely nothing to do with—might be in his house, but at least he had his cologne in his possession.

"Does he do that a lot?" said Steve's father.

"Do what?" said Kelly.

"Lock himself in the bathroom like that."

Steve's father was not particularly good at receiving compliments, so when Kelly told him his boats were "darling," he unconsciously attempted to change the subject.

Kelly sighed. "No. I mean, not until this week, at least. Unfortunately, there's been a lot of shutting ourselves in the bathroom lately. I did it the other day myself. I know you just got here, and it's so good to finally meet you, but to be completely honest, Steve and I are going through a tough time."

Steve's father nodded. Even though he'd been married to a wonderful woman at one point, they'd experienced their fair share of rough patches. He also wasn't surprised that Steve hadn't joined him and Kelly at the kitchen table. After all, his son had spent decades writing him letters specifically stating he didn't want to see him.

"Well," said Steve's father with a smile, "I guess that gives you and I more time to catch up."

Now Kelly smiled. She never quite understood why Steve was

always so mad at his father. Steve had told her that he was a pharmacist and that he wouldn't let him eat in diners and that he wouldn't let him wear a baseball glove, but were those things really *that* bad? At least Steve *had* a father. Kelly never had any kind of fatherly influence growing up.

So, although moments ago Kelly had been ready to get in her car and drive as far away from Steve as possible, she now felt like sitting in her kitchen and getting to know her long-lost father-in-law.

"How long have you been painting boats?"

"Oh, for quite a while. Ever since Steve was a child. We had an unfortunate family incident at one of his baseball games when he was a boy, and ever since that day, I started painting tiny wooden boats. Something about getting kicked in the groin in public can make you reevaluate things."

"Oh," said Kelly. Steve had never told her that story. "I'm sorry to hear you got kicked in the groin in public, but I'm glad that something good came from it."

"Yes," said Steve's father. "Something very good came from it."

Kelly glanced at the coffeemaker and remembered she'd just brewed a fresh pot.

"I'm sorry," she said. "Can I offer you some coffee?"

"No, thank you. I swore an oath when I became a pharmacist that I would never get sick and I would never drink coffee."

"Oh," said Kelly. "I didn't realize you weren't allowed to do those things if you wanted to become a pharmacist. I have to admit that when you dropped in like this, I thought maybe you were here to tell Steve you had a terminal illness or something."

Steve's father laughed. "Me? Get a terminal illness? Nope, not going to happen!"

Now that they were talking about pharmacists, Steve's father really came alive. After all these years, his enthusiasm for being a pharmacist hadn't waned one bit. He told Kelly about the pressure he was constantly under, but how he was able to make it through even the darkest times because he possessed the three traits that every pharmacist needed to have in order to be successful: ingenuity, courage, and a tremendous amount of self-respect.

He then told Kelly that he'd recently retired and had over two million dollars in his bank account.

"If you become a pharmacist," said Steve's father, "they guarantee you will retire with at least two million dollars."

"Wow," said Kelly. "That's a lot of money!"

Steve's father beamed with pride. His passion for being a pharmacist was rubbing off on Kelly and now Kelly was wondering if maybe she could become one herself. She told Steve's father that she had ingenuity, courage, and a tremendous amount of self-respect, and that if it was required, she too could give up coffee and never get sick again.

"I think you should pursue it," said Steve's father. "It's never too late to become the person you were meant to be."

"You don't think I'm too old?"

"No one's too old to become a pharmacist!"

It certainly was appealing, the thought of becoming a pharmacist. Kelly liked the idea of having at least two million dollars when she retired, and if she left Steve—as she was pretty sure she was planning to do—she would need to earn money somehow. Maybe this career opportunity was God opening a window.

"If you like," said Steve's father, "I can put in a good word for you."

"That would be incredible!" said Kelly.

Something occurred to Steve's father and his tone suddenly turned serious. "I doubt they'd bring it up, but…"

"What?" said Kelly.

Steve's father took a deep breath and exhaled. "Your time working as a diner waitress might be an issue. That's all. But we'll worry about that when and if we need to."

Kelly shifted in her seat. "I don't understand. What does that have to do with anything?"

"Well," said Steve's father, "as a pharmacist, we're required to consider the welfare of humanity. We're supposed to prevent human suffering to the best of our abilities. And if you served food at a diner, that food was most likely not made with love, and could very well have been made with hate. I know that was your past, and when you held that position, you weren't thinking that someday you might become a pharmacist. Because if you'd had aspirations to become a pharmacist back then, you might not have taken the diner job in the first place. And there's a chance the powers that be might view your waitressing experience as a time when you were *increasing* human suffering, as opposed to preventing it. And if they do ultimately see it that way, they might not take too kindly to the idea of you becoming a pharmacist."

Steve's father could feel himself tensing up. He'd known for a long time that Kelly had been a waitress. Not long after Kelly and Steve were married, Steve sent his father a letter that read:

Dear Dad,

I hope this letter finds you well.
I wanted you to know that I am now a married man.
I married a waitress. Her name is Kelly.
I met her at one of the many, many diners I have eaten at recently.
She is very beautiful.
Not bad for a pine rider, eh?
I'm incredibly happy.
We have no plans to visit you anytime soon.

Regards,
Steve

When he wrote the letter, Steve knew his father would be irate to learn that Steve had married an employee of a diner. And he was. He was furious for years. Even after Steve let his father know that Kelly had left her position as a waitress, it never gave him any peace of mind. To Steve's father, the damage had been done. His son had married someone who didn't care whether or not the food they served was made with love. And that was something that could never be undone.

"When I worked at that diner," said Kelly, becoming slightly defensive, "I made every effort to serve food made with love."

Steve's father sneered. He knew it wasn't polite to sneer at his daughter-in-law so soon after having just met her, but he couldn't help himself. Something about diners had always made him livid.

"So you can honestly say that you never once served food made with hate?" said Steve's father. "Because these are the things they're going to ask you if you want to become a pharmacist and you better get your story straight."

Kelly's mind immediately returned to the time when that man sent his eggs back five times. He certainly hadn't received food made with love. Would it be fair to say that his food was made with *hate*, though? His meal was certainly made with frustration, possibly even annoyance, but *hate*?

And that had only happened one time.

In her heart, Kelly knew that she always brought integrity and absolute professionalism to her position as a diner waitress, and if the board of pharmaceutical directors (or whatever they were called) ever pressed her on the subject, she knew she would pass whatever rigorous line of questioning they threw at her.

Until that time came, however, she didn't feel the need to defend her past actions, especially to a father-in-law who she'd never met until just a few minutes ago and whose opinion she didn't value particularly highly anyway, even if he did happen to have two million in the bank and possessed ingenuity, courage, and a tremendous amount of self-respect.

Kelly looked at the little wooden boats. "Well, they certainly are darling boats," she said. "Thank you again."

She then stood up. "If you'll excuse me now, I need to get some air. Help yourself to anything you like."

The expression on Steve's father's face immediately turned

from disdain to absolute delight. "Now you're thinking like a pharmacist! Fresh air has always been good for the welfare of humanity. Go enjoy it!"

"Thank you," said Kelly. "I will."

As Kelly walked away, Steve's father realized he'd been more than a little brash. Was it really necessary for him to have badgered Kelly about her waitressing history? He might have driven his son away by impressing his high standards of excellence upon him, but he wasn't going to do the same with his daughter-in-law.

"Kelly," he said. "I'm sorry if I came on strong just now. It's just, when I was a pharmacist, I was constantly under pressure—*tremendous* amounts of pressure. And even though I'm retired now, I sometimes still feel that pressure, even though I know that technically it isn't there anymore. I apologize if I took it out on you."

Kelly nodded. "It's okay."

"And," said Steve's father, "I'll let you in on a little secret. I got my pilot's license recently, and if you and Steve play your cards right, I'll take you both on a private flight over the Hoover Dam!"

Kelly smiled and then made her way to the front door. She needed to get out of the house. She'd get some air, clear her head, then come back home, pack her belongings, and then maybe stay at a motel indefinitely.

She just had to get away from her inane husband and his homicidal scheming for a while. And now Steve's father was in their home for reasons that still weren't clear to her, and he possessed his own brand of lunacy, although Kelly did have to admit that Steve's father was the one who'd given her the idea to perhaps become a pharmacist, and for that she would always be grateful to him.

As she walked outside, Kelly decided she was done with men—all men—for the time being. If she never spoke to another man again, it would be too soon.

That was when she spotted Eric sitting in his car. He smiled and waved to her.

Kelly slowly raised her hand and waved back. A moment ago

she might have decided she was done with men for the time being, but she never said she couldn't wave to one.

30

After moving out of Kelly's mother's house, Steve and Kelly drove east for two days. On the second day, they exited the interstate to get gas and found themselves in a suburb that instantly appealed to the both of them.

As Steve filled the tank, he looked around and saw a grocery store, a hardware store, two promising-looking hair salons, a bar, a liquor store, what appeared to be a recently-built elementary school, a Chinese restaurant, and a Pizza Munch.

Steve got back in the car. "I don't feel like driving anymore."

"Me either," said Kelly.

And so it was decided: this would be the place where they made their home.

Locating the town's secret lumberjack society proved more difficult than Steve had bargained for.

After refueling, Steve and Kelly drove over to the bar. Steve thought for sure that whoever ran the bar would be able to point him in the right direction since bars were usually good sources for that type of information.

So Steve and Kelly walked into the bar and ordered two beers.

As Steve handed the bartender cash for the beers, he said, "You wouldn't happen to know where a former lumberjack could find work around here, do you?"

The bartender smiled. His name was Ernie and he had perfectly white teeth. Steve was immediately struck by how white they were, as he had never before seen a bartender with such white teeth. Ernie had worked at the bar for a long time, and even though the owner didn't pay him much money and the tips were lousy, he showed up to work every day in part because he loved hearing the jokes the customers would tell him. That was one thing he could always count on in his line of work—once people started drinking, they'd start telling jokes.

Ernie had heard a thousand different jokes over the years, maybe even two thousand. And now here was Steve, a man he'd never met before, who was about to lay one on him. Ernie hoped it would be a joke he hadn't heard before.

"I give up," said Ernie. "Where?"

By not answering his question directly, Steve figured the bartender was testing him. It made sense; if there was indeed a secret lumberjack society in this town, no one who belonged to it was just going to come out and immediately admit to its existence.

Steve figured he better grease the wheels a little.

"Listen," said Steve. "I just gave you a twenty-dollar bill, and the change is yours to keep. Now I don't know how this works. Is there a code word or something?"

Ernie was beginning to find this situation to be very peculiar. He definitely had not heard this joke before, and now this customer was offering him a suspiciously large tip. Ernie was used to receiving lousy tips, not large tips, and he wasn't sure if this customer really wanted him to keep the tip or if it was just part of the joke.

At any rate, in these types of situations where the joke was simply way over his head, Ernie had learned it was best to just come clean and let the joke teller know that he or she had outsmarted him.

Ernie held his hands up in mock surrender and smiled from ear to ear. "Okay, you got me. *Is* there a code word?"

It was clear to Steve that this bartender wasn't going to give up the location of the lumberjack society without a fight, but he persisted. "I don't know if there's a code word. That's why I'm asking you and that's why I'm offering you this sizeable tip. Now is this something you can help me with or not?"

Out of the one or two thousand jokes Ernie had heard over the years, he was pretty sure this was the worst one anyone had ever tried to tell him. But that didn't prevent Ernie from slapping his hand on the bar and laughing like a hyena for a good thirty seconds.

"Good one!" he said after his laughter subsided and he wiped a tear from his eye. "I'm gonna remember that one."

Ernie knew that one of the reasons customers came back to a given bar and became regulars there was because the bartenders at those bars laughed at their jokes. Most of these customers couldn't get people in the outside world to laugh at their jokes, so they would instead go to bars where their jokes were appreciated by good-natured bartenders. And if sometimes Ernie had to fake that appreciation, so be it. Because if there was one thing Ernie knew the owner of the bar liked, it was regulars. And more regulars meant better job security for Ernie.

Ernie opened the cash register and made change from the twenty-dollar bill Steve had given him. (Obviously that "keep the change" offer had been a part of the customer's odd attempt at humor.) He set the change on the bar and Steve begrudgingly took most of it. He left a little of it for Ernie—just enough to make for a lousy tip.

"Much obliged," said Ernie as he scooped up Steve's lousy tip.

Steve and Kelly then moved to a table and drank their beers in silence.

After they finished their beers, they ate dinner at the Chinese restaurant Steve had noticed while pumping gas. Steve tried to grease the wheels there, too, by offering the server a sizeable tip for information about the town's secret lumberjack society. But the server didn't know (or at least pretended not to know) about any such society. Steve had to think the server was telling the truth, otherwise why would he turn down such a sizeable tip? No one in their right mind who knew the location of the secret lumberjack society would refuse the kind of tip Steve was offering.

They didn't have a place to stay, and neither Steve nor Kelly felt like sleeping in their car, so they got a room at a nearby motel. The motel looked like it had been there for some time and had never been renovated. There was a pool, but it didn't look like the kind of pool you'd want to swim in. In fact, it didn't even look like the kind of pool you'd want to sunbathe by. It basically looked like the kind of pool that you were best off ignoring.

All the driving they'd done had worn Kelly out, and she fell asleep the minute her head hit the pillow. Steve couldn't sleep, though. He knew he and Kelly only had enough money to last another two weeks or so, and if one of them didn't find employment soon, they'd... well, Steve didn't want to entertain that outcome.

The manager of the motel had been just as unhelpful as the bartender and the server at the Chinese restaurant when Steve had told him he was a former lumberjack looking for work. Steve noticed the manager did not have a tip jar, and not only did Steve offer to make him a tip jar, Steve also told him he'd be the first one to put a tip in the jar, and that it would be a substantial tip at that. And all the manager had to do was tell Steve how to find the town's former lumberjacks.

The manager could not have been less interested in Steve's proposition.

"I've got a tip for *you*," the manager said. "Checkout's at eleven."

He then handed Steve the key and that was that.

As Steve lay in bed with his mind racing and his young wife sleeping next to him, his thoughts drifted to a time when his life was simpler and he still lived with his pharmacist father. He recalled the occasions when he would open his bedroom window and speak to the thirty-foot oak tree he called "mom." He remembered feeling a stronger connection with his mother the tree than he'd ever felt with his human dad. She never judged him, never told him he couldn't eat at a diner, never forbade him from wearing a baseball glove, never labeled him a "pine rider." She accepted him for who he was, and he never felt defensive or self-conscious when he was in her presence. He and his mother might not have been able to talk to each other in the conventional sense, but that didn't mean they weren't able to communicate.

When Steve decided to leave home and become a lumberjack, he knew he wouldn't miss his father, but he knew for a fact he would miss that tree.

He wished that tree was still outside his window as he got up and gazed out at the very limited view the motel window had to offer. But there was no thirty-foot oak. There was just the pool that everyone ignored, and then way off in the distance, the sign for the gas station where Steve had fueled up earlier in the day.

Steve hadn't paid much attention to the clerk at the gas station at the time; he was too busy falling in love with his new surroundings and daydreaming about his and his wife's future there. But now that he thought about it, the clerk wore an eye patch, he moved around with a limp, and one of his arms appeared to be lame. Clearly, this man had either been hit by a bus at some point in his life, or he'd gotten his ass kicked by lumberjacks.

Steve was hoping it was the latter as he quickly threw on some clothes, kissed his sleeping wife on her head, and raced out the door.

31

Steve heard Kelly leave the house. He had no idea where she was going or if she'd be returning anytime soon. He'd initially attempted to eavesdrop on the conversation she was having with his father, but he'd found it difficult to hear them through the bathroom door and eventually gave up trying.

As he sat in the hallway bathroom with the door securely locked, he knew he was now alone in his house with his father. He felt silly sitting in the bathroom—especially *this* bathroom, the hallway bathroom, his least favorite bathroom in the house.

This was *his* house after all and if he didn't want his father to be there, he had every right to kick him out.

Steve had his phone with him and thought this might be a good opportunity for him to catch up with close friends he hadn't spoken to in a while. Then he remembered he didn't have any close friends; he didn't really have any friends at all these days. Not even distant ones.

So instead he called the two men to see if they now had a progress report for him. He'd paid them the extra money they'd requested, so he had to imagine things were finally in the works. Even if for whatever reason things were not in the works, at least he could confirm with them that they received the additional eight hundred dollars.

The two men were outside the gym smoking with Chester Rawlings when the first man's cell phone rang. He saw the number on the caller ID and recognized it as Steve's. He was in no mood to talk to Steve; he was having too much fun smoking cigarettes with his brother and Chester Rawlings.

Neither the first man nor his brother had smoked a cigarette in twelve years, and neither would have predicted their day would have turned out like this—that they would get to know Chester Rawlings, discover that he was the same age as one of them, not kill him, and then start smoking again.

Chester had given each of the men a cigarette. It was a special kind of cigarette where if you wanted it to taste like a regular cigarette, you just lit it and smoked it. But if you wanted it to taste like a menthol cigarette, you squeezed the filter really hard and that released some chemicals that would transform it into a menthol cigarette.

Both men were smoking their cigarettes with the regular flavor and both men were observing Chester's popularity. Everyone who walked into the gym waved to Chester and not one single person— not even the parents who had their kids with them—objected to Chester's smoking or made any kind of face that remotely expressed disapproval.

One of the gym patrons even bummed a cigarette from Chester as she left the gym following her Pilates class. She introduced herself to the men as Daphne. She was a bubbly young woman in a sweat suit and told Chester the Pilates class had "really kicked her ass" and that she was "totally dying" for a cigarette.

Daphne smiled at the two men as she walked away. The two brothers shared a look with each other that seemed to say that they were leaning toward joining this gym, especially if there were more young women like Daphne who went there and who, like Daphne, also enjoyed smoking cigarettes immediately following their workout.

The first man now stepped away from Chester and his brother to take Steve's call.

"Yeah," he said.

"Hey," said Steve. "What's the latest?"

"We're working on it."

"Okay, okay. Did you get the eight hundred?"

"Yeah, we got the eight hundred."

"Good."

"There was a problem, though."

"A problem? What kind of problem?"

In actuality, there had been no problem, but the man was quite upset that Steve was cutting into his smiling time. The man was also remembering how much he disliked smoking while talking on the phone. When he used to smoke he liked to either just smoke or just talk on the phone. He couldn't stand doing both at the same time.

It wasn't Steve's fault that he caught the man before he finished his cigarette, but that still didn't make the man any less pissed off.

"Yeah, a big problem," said the man. "You paper-clipped the money. We specifically told you to put the money in an envelope."

Steve couldn't believe what he was hearing. "What? What does that have to do with anything? You *got* the money! And not only that, you told me you were going to call me after you got it. Where's the fucking communication? Why am I the one doing all the work here?"

The man took a last drag from his cigarette, dropped it on the ground, and stubbed it out with his shoe. He briefly thought about what kind of cigarettes he'd buy at the liquor store later in the day, now that he was smoking again. He also wondered what color lighter he'd purchase. He was thinking red—classic and simple. The image of him using his red lighter to light the cigarette of a pretty young woman who had just finished her Pilates class and was totally dying for a cigarette popped in his head. He wanted to think about that image some more, but first he had to deal with Steve.

"Listen, you clown. Do you want this to go smoothly or not?"

"Of course I want it to go smoothly!"

"Then you're going to have to shut the fuck up and let us do our job."

Steve was not a big fan of letting people do their jobs. Steve liked to be the one in control. He was doing his best to see things from the point of view of the two men, but he was also paying them good money and therefore felt strongly that he should have significant influence over how and when the job was done.

"I don't appreciate your tone, and I still don't think it's unreasonable to request the occasional update," said Steve.

"Be that as it may," said the man, "we'll contact you when it's time to talk. So if you don't hear from us, that means it's not time to talk. Do you understand?"

On a normal day, this was the point where Steve would have gone ballistic. He would have screamed at the man and let him know that he would not be jerked around. He would have reminded him in no uncertain terms that he had made that last drop out of protest, and that whether or not the cash was in an envelope was completely irrelevant as the men had acknowledged receipt of the money, *so who cares whether the money was in an envelope or not?*

It's also highly likely that Steve would have then called the man a horrible name, thrown his phone at the bathroom mirror, ripped the tank cover off the toilet and repeatedly smacked the countertop with it. He then would have kicked something (most likely the toilet) so hard that it would have broken his big toe, or at least bruised it severely.

But this was not a normal day. Steve's estranged father was in his house, and Steve did not want his father to think that there was any drama or strife in his life whatsoever. He wanted his father to think that his was a life that was disciplined, orderly, perhaps even methodical.

In other words, throwing a hissy fit in the hallway bathroom was not something Steve wanted his father to overhear. So instead, he took the high road with the man—or at least, a version of the high road.

"You know," said Steve, as cool as a cucumber, "after I made that drop out of protest, I went into Pizza Munch and I ate a pizza. And I had a very pretty young lady serve me, and I asked her if I looked good for fifty-two. And she told me I *did.*"

"The hell do I care?" said the man. He was getting really sick of this conversation.

"I'm telling you this, because when we first met the other day, you told me I looked *dead.* But I don't. I look damn good for my age and I've got pretty young ladies confirming that for me all the time."

Then Steve hung up.

The man smirked when he heard the click. This Steve guy was something else. The man thought about how Steve had said he was fifty-two, which happened to be his brother's age. If his brother had been the one on the phone with Steve just now, it's quite possible that Steve and his brother would have bonded over being the same age.

But since the man Steve was talking to was fifty-four, he and Steve didn't bond, and the man decided it wasn't worth telling his fifty-two-year-old brother that Steve was also fifty-two.

He walked back to his younger brother and Chester, who were smiling and finishing their cigarettes. Now that the man was no longer talking to Steve on the phone, he started smiling again, too.

"Everything good?" said the second man.

"Everything's good."

Chester put his cigarette out in the ashtray and extended his hand. "It was nice meeting you gentlemen, but I've gotta get back to it. Let me know what you decide about the memberships."

One of the perks of being brothers and spending a lot of time together is that you tend to know what the other one is thinking at all times. So as the brothers shook Chester's hand, they looked at each other with knowing grins.

"Hey," said the first man, "does that ten percent discount offer still stand if we sign a one-year contract today?"

"You better believe it does," said Chester.

"Good," said the second man. "Because we're in."

And just like that, the two men walked back into the gym with Chester to make their memberships official. They might have initially visited the gym to put a bullet in Chester's brain, but instead they were now becoming gym members, smiling more than they ever had at any point in their lives, and smoking again for the first time in twelve years.

If only they'd brought their bathing suits with them, maybe they would have topped the day off with a swim.

32

Kelly was sitting on a couch in Eric's living room. It was an exceedingly white room. The walls were white and most of the furniture was white. It was a clean room. There was no clutter. It was clear to Kelly that Eric was the type of man who believed that there was a place for everything, and everything had a place, or whatever the expression was.

She noticed a telescope by the large picture window. The telescope was also white.

Eric walked into the living room holding two champagne flutes. He handed one to Kelly and sat down on the couch next to her. They clinked glasses and each took a sip. They did not make a toast.

When Kelly spotted Eric sitting in his car outside her house, she walked up to his Saturn and Eric rolled down the passenger side window and invited her to get in.

Kelly got in and then the two of them sat in silence for a moment. Eric's heart was racing. He was finally back in Kelly's company. He had so many things to say to her, so many passionate feelings to confess. But there were too many thoughts swirling around in his head and he wasn't sure which thought to trust, and it had been so long since he'd expressed romantic feelings to a woman and this was a married woman on top of it and he didn't want to say the wrong thing, but he wasn't sure what the right thing to say was, either. So he simply said, "Do you want to get a drink?"

It was quite early in the morning. It was not the time of day when people normally went out to get a drink. He immediately regretted asking it. He knew Kelly would now think he was some type of drunk, or an animal, or a drunken animal. Shit, for all he knew, she probably thought he was a serial killer for having asked a question like that.

But the question had been asked. It was out there now, and there was nothing that Eric could do except wait for Kelly to respond.

To Eric's surprise, and relief, Kelly actually nodded. Initially it was a slow nod as she stared straight ahead, looking out the windshield. But then she turned to look at Eric as she continued to nod, and gave him a half smile.

Eric returned Kelly's half smile with a half smile of his own. Actually, his was closer to a full smile. He then started the car and drove.

It didn't occur to Eric to tell Kelly that they were going to his house. Normally, Eric knew it was customary for the male to ask the female where she might like to go to have the drink. Alternatively, sometimes the male would simply say, "I know a place," and drive them both there. Usually the drink was had at a bar or a restaurant, and then if things were going well, at that point, either the male or the female might suggest that they go back to one of their homes.

But Eric and Kelly skipped that step. There was no discussion as to where they would have their drink. In fact, there was no discussion at all. They didn't say a word to each other during the drive to Eric's house. They didn't say a word as they entered Eric's house. And they didn't say a word just now as they toasted.

For whatever reason, the silence wasn't uncomfortable, and Kelly was enjoying the peace, since she'd had so little of it recently.

Eric had poured them mimosas. Champagne again. It seemed

Kelly couldn't avoid it lately. She'd drunk two bottles of it by herself yesterday, and then last night Steve had told her he wanted to take her out for a glass of champagne to toast his impending homicide.

"Do you normally drink this early in the day?" said Kelly.

"Never," said Eric. He was glad Kelly asked him that question so he could clear his name as it were, and let her know that this was abnormal behavior for him and he was not, in fact, a serial killer. "I'm sorry—I just got tongue-tied and didn't know what else to say."

"It's fine," said Kelly. "Even if you do."

"Well, I don't," said Eric as politely as possible. "I can promise you that."

Usually when two people drank during the day, it was important for neither person to ask the other any serious questions regarding their drinking habits that might imply that one person thought the other drank too much, because if either party thought the other was judging their alcohol consumption, it could really put a damper on things.

This unspoken rule also pertained to two people who drank together at night, but at night, if one implied the other drank too much, it could be laughed off easier, and there was a much lesser chance that any actual feelings would be hurt.

But drinking during the day was a whole different thing. People were much more sensitive about it. Whereas if you drank too much at night, you *might* have a drinking problem, but if you drank too much during the day, then you *definitely* had a drinking problem, unless you were in a city where drinking during the day was socially acceptable, like Paris or Lake Tahoe.

Eric wasn't sure if Kelly believed that he didn't normally drink so early in the day. He was hurt that she might not trust him, but he also had to admit he hadn't really given her much of a reason to trust him in the first place. He and Kelly had made out hard, and then he just up and disappeared on her, and next thing you know he's showing up at her house uninvited and asking her to come back to his place for a drink after not having spoken to her in days. If there was a way for him to have fucked up this courting of Kelly any further than he already had, he sure couldn't think of it. What a weirdo he was. What a strange, strange person. What a loser. What an imbecile. What an ass. What a waste of life. What a sad sack. What a...

"Are you thinking negative thoughts?" said Kelly.

Eric was busted and he knew it. He also knew Kelly was going to remind him that they learned in their compliments class that one negative thought negated three compliments. Ugh. He was the worst host who'd ever lived. He'd invited Kelly to his house only to sit next to her on his couch and think negative thoughts. *What kind of person behaves like this?* thought Eric. He didn't want to answer that question, though, because in his heart he knew what kind of person behaved like that: a serial killer.

Eric came clean. "Yes, I was thinking negative thoughts. You're very astute."

Kelly smiled. "That's okay. You should have seen me yesterday. I was drowning in negative thoughts. If I'd counted them all, I think I would have ended up with negative five thousand compliments for the day!"

"I missed you."

"I missed you, too."

"I'm sorry I gave you that flower. I know that put you in a tough position."

"It's okay. I ate it."

"You ate it?"

"Yes. It was a violet. They're edible."

Kelly and Eric finished their mimosas.

"Do you want another one?" said Eric.

Kelly did want another one, but she also didn't want Eric to think she normally drank so early in the day, so she avoided the question by asking a question of her own.

"Eric," she said. "Do you think you suffer from compliment overconfidence?"

Eric scoffed. "What? Of course not. Where did you get that idea?"

"From Jennifer. She said that's why you dropped the course—because you felt you'd mastered complimenting and knew everything there was to know about the craft. It really is okay if you feel that way. You're one of the best complimenters I've ever met. You definitely have genius in that area."

Eric laughed. "I don't think I've ever felt overconfident about anything a day in my life! But I thank you for the compliment. I didn't know you thought of me as one of the best complimenters you ever met."

Even though she still barely knew him, Kelly had come to admire that quality about Eric—his ability to accept a compliment. Not only could he give them out, but he could graciously accept them, too. He wouldn't try to deflect the compliment or tell Kelly she was full of shit. He simply acknowledged it and expressed his gratitude for having received it.

Kelly also thought about how before Eric had abandoned their class, she'd envisioned herself traveling the world with him as he spoke at compliments seminars and they would drink champagne and stay up all night complimenting each other until sunrise.

Maybe they weren't exactly traveling the world together, and maybe Eric didn't have any compliments-related speaking engagements lined up in the near future, but all the same, here they were drinking champagne. Some of her fantasy was coming true!

"I'm sorry I left the class," said Eric. "And this is difficult for me to say to you, but you deserve to hear the truth." Eric really wanted another mimosa, but, like Kelly, he didn't want to risk being judged for drinking too much too early in the day. He would have to tell her what he had to say without the further assistance of liquid courage.

"I took the class to meet women. I mean, not a *lot* of women. I took the class to hopefully meet *a* woman. And I did. I met you. And you're… you're amazing, but you're also, you know, *married*. And it's a compliments class and not an adultery class and I apologize if I led you on. I didn't mean for this to happen. I didn't mean for this to happen this way."

Kelly hadn't meant for this to happen, either. But it was happening nonetheless.

"My husband already thinks I'm having an affair," said Kelly.

"Why does he think that?" said Eric.

"Because I told him I was having one. Or at least I told him it was trending in the direction of an affair."

Eric couldn't believe what he was hearing. "*Why did you tell him that?*"

"We were having an argument."

Eric remembered what it was like to be married and have arguments. Before his wife died in the freak swing set accident, they would argue constantly. That was before they stopped communicating and stopped having sex, but prior to that, they would quarrel with great regularity. And the things they would say to each other during those altercations were nasty, frightful, and always off-putting.

So Eric didn't hold it against Kelly for telling her husband that she might be having an affair. If anything, this excited Eric. It seemed as if Kelly was experiencing the same wolf love he'd been feeling.

He pulled Kelly toward him and kissed her lips. They started making out hard. Eric wondered if perhaps he was moving too fast for Kelly. Maybe he should have first offered to freshen her drink again, or he could have put on a pot of coffee, or if she was a tea drinker, he could have offered to make her tea. Or maybe she was hungry. He could have suggested that he whip up some delicious avocado toast. He had those two avocados that were close to going bad. If he didn't use them in the next day or two, he'd have to throw them out. And he hated—absolutely hated—throwing out food. Especially avocados. Why did he always buy so many at once? He never used them all in time, and then he'd feel guilty for having wasted them.

But thoughts of further drinking, avocado toast, and

squandered food soon drifted from Eric's mind as Kelly began un-zipping his pants and Eric decided it would be best to focus on the present moment instead.

33

There weren't many positive things that could be said for the gas station. The gas pumps had seen better days, there were no windshield squeegees anywhere in sight, and the bathroom was outside and didn't even have a door. There was just a curtain that you pulled across if you wanted privacy. And the curtain wasn't exactly fresh out of the box, either.

The gas station was well-lit, however. As Steve approached it, he thought to himself it might be one of the better-lit gas stations he'd ever seen in his life. The fluorescents were dazzling, and Steve couldn't spot a single burnt-out bulb. Whoever was in charge of the lighting had clearly brought their A-game.

The same couldn't be said for whoever was in charge of the rest of the place, though. Steve gave the front door a good tug with both hands as he entered the convenience store portion of the gas station. He remembered from earlier in the day when he'd filled his tank there that the door stuck, and he recalled thinking at the time that senior citizens and small children probably had a difficult time opening it. It wasn't a particularly easy door to work with, and was yet another item at the gas station that desperately needed improvement.

He immediately found the man he was looking for. He was sitting behind the counter with his back to Steve. His face was pressed close to a little black-and-white TV. President Reagan was speaking, and the man seemed to be hanging on Reagan's every word.

"Excuse me," said Steve.

The man didn't respond. He was really interested in whatever it was Regan was talking about. Steve didn't want to be rude, so he just stood there and waited for the man to finish watching Regan's speech. This was at a time in Steve's life when Steve was still relatively patient and considerate of others, so it didn't bother him too much to be ignored.

As Steve stood there being ignored, he took the opportunity to let his eyes roam around the store. He noticed there wasn't much of a candy bar selection. There were only three different kinds of candy bars, and none of them were the kind that Steve would be interested in eating anyway. Steve thought about how if he were a kid, he would have been very disappointed by this store's offerings. He also noticed an absence of baseball cards. What kind of gas station didn't sell baseball cards?

On the wall behind the cash register, there were several varieties of cigarettes on display, as well as a few packs of C-cell batteries, and what appeared to be a bag of beef jerky. Other than that, the wall was bare and badly in need of a paint job.

Reagan must have finished his speech, because the clerk turned off his TV and turned to Steve.

"Can I help you?"

There was really no getting around it—the clerk was not a handsome man. In addition to his eye patch, he had crooked teeth that were approaching the color brown, his eyes were uneven as the right eye plainly hung lower than the left, and his long, gray, straw-like hair appeared to have not been washed in a decade.

In that moment, Steve did not want the clerk's help all that much. He wanted to turn around and leave the store. Steve had seen some pretty haggard-looking men during his time working as a lumberjack/office worker, but this was something else entirely: the clerk's appearance was downright repellent.

Although every fiber of his being told him to flee, what other options did Steve have? He and Kelly had very little money between them and no place to live. If they didn't get something cooking immediately, they would have to either go live with Steve's father (which was definitely not an option), go live with Kelly's mother (also definitely not an option), or get ready to start living in Kelly's car. And for Steve, at least, that was not an option, either, as he equated people who lived in cars with pine riders and since Steve took great pride in *not* being a pine rider, that meant that potentially living in Kelly's car was not an option, either.

So Steve sucked it up and addressed the creepy clerk.

"Are you a lumberjack?"

"Who wants to know?"

"I do. Just me."

The clerk's name was Glen and he had indeed been a lumberjack. He'd been a lumberjack for over seventeen years. And he'd been pretty good at it, too. He was by no means the best lumberjack that had ever lived, but he was by no means the worst, either.

Like Steve, circumstances had forced Glen into a situation where he had to either accept a transfer, or retire and fight the entire company at once.

Like Steve, Glen had chosen the latter.

And just like Steve, Glen had found himself on the road, looking for a new home, before arbitrarily stopping in this sleepy town and settling down.

At least now the town had a Chinese restaurant and a bar and a Pizza Munch. When Glen had arrived, it didn't even have those things. They'd also recently built an elementary school, and Glen had also heard rumors about a new shopping mall that was going to be built any year now, as well as two new, state-of-the-art gas stations that were supposedly going to offer their customers a wide selection of candy and fountain drinks.

Sometimes Glen worried about how the new gas stations might affect his business. He knew his candy selection was lacking and he didn't offer any fountain drinks at all. If those other gas stations were eventually constructed, he was well aware that he would have to make major improvements in the candy and beverage departments, and he'd probably also have to finally get around to putting a real door on the bathroom—and not just any old door, but a door that locked, too. And those kinds of doors could be very expensive.

Glen wasn't getting any younger, either. It was becoming more and more difficult for him to run the gas station by himself. He found his concentration wasn't what it used to be. For example, here was a young man standing in front of him, who had just asked him a question, but for whatever reason, Glen couldn't recall for the life of him what that question was. In these situations, Glen assumed that it was simply another salesperson trying to sell him something he didn't need, so he said to Steve what he said to salespeople whenever they pestered him: "Thank you, but I'm not interested." He then turned his back to Steve and switched on his little TV.

What is with this town? thought Steve. Why was everyone being so coy as to the whereabouts of the secret lumberjack society? Granted, it was supposed to be a secret. Steve understood that part. But after a certain point, if no one offered any information at all— not even a clue, or a hint, or even a suggestion—then how were recently-retired lumberjacks supposed to locate the societies, and how were they ever supposed to find work again?

"Listen," said Steve, "I don't care if you want a sizeable tip. Hell, I'll just give you whatever cash I have left. But I need work. I need to know if there's a secret lumberjack society in this town and I need to know like right fucking now."

Aha! thought Glen. That's what Steve had asked him. He'd asked him if he was a lumberjack. It was all coming back now.

"Yes," said Glen with great enthusiasm. "I do know about the secret lumberjack society."

Steve couldn't believe it. He was finally getting somewhere. "Great! Where is it?"

"You're looking at it," said Glen.

To say Steve was incredibly disappointed would have been an understatement. Glen was disappointed, too. But Glen's disappointment was disappointment in himself. No one had ever asked him about the secret lumberjack society before and he wasn't sure whether he was supposed to come out and acknowledge its existence as quickly as he'd just done, or whether he should have kept things hush-hush.

Damn, he hadn't even checked with Steve first to verify that Steve was a lumberjack. It's quite possible he really screwed the pooch on this one. He might very well have just given up the existence of the secret lumberjack society to someone who wasn't even a lumberjack. If only there was a rulebook, or a person Glen could consult with in this type of situation to get an official ruling.

Meanwhile, Steve was wondering what exactly Glen had meant when he said, "You're looking at it." Was Glen saying he was literally the only member of the secret lumberjack society? A one-person secret lumberjack society? What the hell kind of society was that?

As the two men stood there, reevaluating the moves they'd just made, and not quite trusting each other, a young boy, probably around the age of seven, attempted to enter the store.

He was having difficulty opening the door, as all boys his age did. He tugged and tugged, using both hands, and all the strength he could muster, but he couldn't get the door to budge.

Neither Glen nor Steve made any attempt to assist him, and the boy eventually gave up and walked away. It was probably for the best. There really wasn't much this gas station had to offer a seven-year-old boy other than excellent lighting, and no seven-year-old boy in the history of seven-year-old boys has ever been particularly interested in lighting.

34

The time Steve spent in the bathroom had been fairly productive. He'd received a progress report from the two men, he'd relieved himself after really having to urinate upon waking up from his latest baleen whale dream, and he'd even splashed some cologne on his face.

As he looked at himself in the mirror, he wasn't thrilled about the idea of leaving the bathroom and having to interact with his father who had absolutely no business being in his home, but at the same time he knew he had the focus and determination to order his father to leave, as well as the courage and willpower to tell him to go fuck himself if need be.

Steve entered the kitchen to find his father sitting at the kitchen table. He was staring out a window, looking at Steve's backyard. Steve then spotted the two wooden boats on the table and an intense anger immediately overtook him. It was an anger he hadn't experienced since that fateful day when he saw his fellow lumberjack Brad with a wooden boat. Steve was temporarily paralyzed with rage.

"Have you ever considered putting in a pool?" said Steve's father. "You have the space for it."

Steve's father then swiveled in his chair and turned his gaze from Steve's backyard to Steve. Steve looked pretty good, he thought. He could have maybe looked a bit better, but overall he wasn't disappointed by what he saw. He stood up to offer his son a handshake, a handshake he hoped might lead to a hug, but he didn't want to come on too strong, so he led with the handshake, and if it was meant to be, he knew a hug would ensue shortly thereafter.

As Steve's father approached him, Steve extended both arms with his palms out to let him know to keep his distance.

"Oh, come on now, Steve, this is getting a bit old, isn't it? I know I was never quite the father you wanted me to be, but I wasn't a deadbeat, either. I taught you valuable life skills..."

Steve's father's voice trailed off as he saw the color of his son's face turning from red to a dark red, to a color he hadn't quite seen before, but it appeared to be bordering on purple. It was a rapid procession of colors, and none of the colors were the types of colors that would normally appear in a person's face, unless that person was experiencing a considerable amount of discomfort.

Steve was so angry he could barely talk, but somehow, through gritted teeth and with a formidable amount of effort he was just able to spit out, "I want you and those boats out of here immediately."

Steve then imagined himself lighting the boats on fire and shoving them down his father's throat while they were still aflame. That's how mad Steve was. He then imagined himself burning his whole house down. And then he imagined the fire spreading to the next house, and to the house after that, and before you knew it, the whole neighborhood would be in flames. And then the fire would extend to other neighborhoods as well until all the neighborhoods on Planet Earth were burned to a crisp.

Something about envisioning all the neighborhoods on Planet Earth being burned to a crisp actually helped Steve calm down. Because in his fantasy, if absolutely everything was burned to a crisp, then what would be left to be angry about anymore? If anything, in that type of scenario, Steve would only have himself to blame as he would have been the one who had caused all that destruction in the first place.

As Steve started to breathe normally again, and as the color of his face began to transition to a healthier-looking hue that was far less purple, he came up with a compromise. No, he would not start any fires and he would not shove any flaming boats down his father's throat. Instead, Steve looked his father in the eye and said this:

"No one invited you here. You are an uninvited person, and this is a situation that I believe could be classified as trespassing. I have no desire to communicate with you, and I certainly have no desire to communicate with you in my house, which is a place where you should not even be standing. However, since you're here today, I have to imagine you have something fairly important to talk to me about, so I will grant you an audience with me, but I will not grant you that audience here in my home. That audience will only be granted at a venue of my choosing. And that venue will be a diner."

The diner part stung. Steve's father was okay with Steve accusing him of trespassing, and he was okay with Steve turning various colors, and he was even okay with Steve ignoring his question about putting in a pool, but the thing about the diner hurt. Good Lord he had a stubborn son. If there was one thing Steve had been consistent with over the years, it was his stubbornness. Anything to stick it to the old man.

Still, when it came to communication with one's children, Steve's father knew you had to take what you could get. And if those were the terms, if he had to go to a disgusting, hate-filled diner in order to talk to his son in person, then so be it.

"Fine," said Steve's father. "I'll drive."

"No," said Steve. "I'll drive. And for the love of God, get those fucking boats out of here."

Steve's father was normally not the kind of person who would elicit any type of sympathy, but even so, it was more than a little sad to watch him pick up the rejected boats he'd spent so much time detailing and perfecting for his son and daughter-in-law.

But Steve had made it abundantly clear: the boats weren't welcome in his house, and neither was he.

35

Eric and Kelly were sitting in bed eating avocado toast. Eric was happy that he was able to use the two avocados before they went bad. He really did despise wasting food. But mostly he was happy to be sitting in bed with Kelly.

Kelly was happy to be sitting in bed with Eric. But she was also happy that she was the one being served. When she was younger and working as a waitress, she was serving people all the time. And when she lived with her mother, she served her meals and drinks all the time there, too. And then her whole life with Steve was just serving him one meal after another and a lot of those times he wasn't grateful for the meal or he complained about it.

But Eric was different. This morning he'd served her champagne, and now he was serving her delicious avocado toast. She could get used to this, she thought.

"I noticed you had a telescope," said Kelly.

"Yes," said Eric. "It's not very powerful. I pretty much use it for décor more than anything."

"Are you into astronomy?"

"Yes…"

Geez, thought Eric. Of all the things in his house that she could have brought up to talk about, why did she have to mention the telescope? He'd bought that telescope for one purpose and one purpose only. And that purpose was to locate Cliff in the sky so that he and Cliff could have a closer connection. How on earth was he going to explain this to Kelly? She would think he was insane.

Of course, parking in front of Kelly's house all night and then offering her alcohol first thing in the morning were also insane things that he'd recently done, and those things had led to sex. So maybe coming clean about his relationship with Cliff wasn't the worst thing he could do?

"I sort of adopted a star," said Eric. "And I talk to it at night. It's sort of like having a pet and it's also like a form of counseling. Cliff has helped me through some difficult times. And he was also the one who encouraged me to take the compliments class and he also encouraged me to drive to your house to tell you how I felt about you."

Kelly set down her avocado toast. Eric worried that what he'd just told her had made her lose her appetite. But then she turned to Eric, put her hand on his face, and smiled at him.

"And how exactly *do* you feel about me?"

Though initially relieved that she wasn't put off by him telling her about his friendship with Cliff, Eric found that to be a somewhat odd question. How could she not know how he felt about her? How could she not know the feelings and the lust that she stirred in him? How could she not know about the fire that burned in him whenever he saw her, or whenever he just thought about her?

Then he realized he'd never really communicated all that to her. Most of it had simply been played out in his mind. Sure, he'd given her a flower and told her that it reminded him of her, and he'd (unintentionally) camped out all night in front of her house, and he'd of course given her many, many compliments since they'd met, but he'd never fully explained to her how he truly felt about her. At least, not until now:

"I have wolf love for you."

Kelly's smile grew even bigger upon hearing those words. She took the plate of avocado toast that Eric was still holding and set it next to her avocado toast.

Then she straddled Eric, and for the next hour or so, they complimented each other with their bodies, instead of using words. This was not a technique that was specifically taught in their class, but that didn't make this particular complimenting session any less pleasurable.

36

Steve and Kelly were having sex in the motel shower. It was the first and only time they attempted shower sex. It went okay, but shower sex can often times be a bit clunky and uncomfortable. It's not the type of sex that's necessarily meant to go on for an extended length of time.

But even though the deck was stacked against them, they still managed to pull off successful shower sex. Afterwards they agreed there were some things about both of their performances that could be fine-tuned so the next time they did it in the shower it would make for an even more satisfying experience.

Steve and Kelly were happy that for the first time since they'd met they were able to have regular, full-on sex. Prior to this, they had to have delicate sex because Steve's body was still very tender as he recovered from the injuries he sustained at the hands of the lumberjacks. Even just a few weeks ago, shower sex would have been completely unthinkable.

In addition to the sex being delicate, it also had to be quiet, because they'd been living with Kelly's mother. Since Kelly's mother was more or less drunk all the time, there's a good chance she never would have heard them anyway, but they figured it wasn't worth taking the risk.

The sex they had at the motel, though, was a whole different ball game. It was varied, it was often loud, and more times than not, it was no-holds-barred.

These were some of the happiest days of Steve and Kelly's lives. Steve was now gainfully employed at the gas station and because Steve was making money, Kelly did not have to work as a waitress.

After their initial awkward encounter, Glen decided to hire Steve. Glen wasn't really sure whether he needed the help or not, but Steve had mentioned he was a lumberjack and Glen remembered something about how lumberjacks were supposed to help one another out through the secret societies, plus Steve had offered Glen all the cash he had left, and that's what really put it over the top. Glen's memory might not have been very good anymore, but he never forgot that he liked money. He never forgot he liked money for one second of his life, no matter how bad his mind got.

Initially, Steve didn't make any money at all working at the gas station because the first week or so he was just earning back all the money he'd given Glen so Glen would hire him in the first place. Fortunately, Kelly had a little extra money that she'd saved from waitressing, so Steve and Kelly were still able to live at the motel.

It didn't take long at all for Steve to make some major improvements to the gas station. He fixed the door so senior citizens and small children would no longer have such a difficult time opening it. After that, he put a fresh coat of paint on the wall behind the cash register.

He also put a door on the bathroom. It was a door with a lock, even. Steve also markedly improved the candy bar selection. Basically overnight, the gas station went from offering three different kinds of candy bars to offering nearly twenty different kinds.

But what Steve was most proud of was that the gas station now sold baseball cards. More kids started coming to the gas station now that they could open the door and now that the gas station sold baseball cards. Steve on occasion gave the kids free packs of cards. He couldn't help it—the baseball cards just made everyone so happy, except for Glen. Glen never really understood what they were. But everyone else loved the baseball cards. One time, one of the kids opened his pack to find a Fernando Valenzuela rookie card. You should have seen the boy's face light up when he saw it. You would have thought he'd just won a million dollars.

It was around this time that Steve and Kelly decided they should leave the motel. They really liked living there and having sex there, but it was also pretty expensive and although they knew they'd be uncomfortable for a while, they decided it was best to live in Kelly's car so they could save up money to buy a house. The suburb they were in was still very new and the houses weren't all that expensive yet, so if they hunkered down and watched their spending, they knew that before too long they could afford a home of their own.

Glen said they could park their car at the gas station and live at the gas station parking lot for as long as they liked. Since the gas station was so well-lit, they always felt safe.

The only drawback about living in Kelly's car was finding a place to have sex. Both Steve and Kelly were still quite young at the time, so sex was very important to them and they wanted to have privacy when they did it. Having sex in a car in a well-lit gas station parking lot wasn't ideal for people who weren't exhibitionists. So instead they would sometimes use the gas station bathroom now that the bathroom had a door that locked, and other times they would do it in the car. On the occasions they had sex in the car, they used the cardboard boxes the baseball cards came in for privacy. Steve collected the boxes, and then Kelly would cut them to size so they perfectly covered all the windows as well as the front and rear windshields. All they had to do was tape them up!

Prior to living in Kelly's car, Steve had always been adamantly opposed to living in cars because he thought only pine riders lived in cars. But Steve was finding that he actually really enjoyed living in a car. Maybe it was because Kelly was with him that made the difference. Maybe it was because the car he lived in was right next to where he worked so he didn't have to deal with rush hour traffic. Maybe it was because he knew that living in Kelly's car wasn't a permanent thing, and the reason they were living in it was because they were working toward something bigger.

Maybe it was a combination of all those things. But whatever it was, during that time Steve would have been perfectly happy working at the gas station and living in Kelly's car for the rest of his life.

37

The two men were standing in the liquor store. They'd come to the liquor store to buy cigarettes and a lighter. They noticed that this particular liquor store had some rather odd specials. If you bought one bottle of champagne, you got three percent off a second bottle. And if you bought a canister of salted peanuts, you got twenty cents off a second canister.

The lackluster liquor store specials really put into perspective what a great deal Chester had given them by allowing them to join the gym at ten percent off.

The younger brother thought to himself that he felt somewhat bad that he and his older brother had given Chester fake IDs when they'd signed off on the memberships. They were beginning to think that Chester might become a friend of theirs, and even though he and his brother currently had no friends, he knew that friends didn't give friends fake IDs when applying for gym memberships at a discounted rate.

But then he remembered that it was for the best that Chester didn't know their real identities anyway, because if he did, then they would most likely have to kill him and they really were doing their best to get out of the killing business.

The men weren't quite sure how they were going to handle the whole Pool Pisser thing. What they did know was that they had already been paid over seven thousand dollars for doing very little work and that Steve was sitting on nearly forty-seven thousand more.

And just because they'd decided they weren't going to kill Chester, that didn't mean they were just going to walk away from the rest of that money. Maybe they would ask Steve if he had any other suspects. Maybe they'd look for the suspects themselves now that they were gym members and could therefore spend as much time as they wanted at the gym every day without raising suspicion.

Or maybe they'd just take the rest of the money from Steve without killing anyone at all.

The men had been put in touch with Steve through a bouncer named Desmond. Steve had placed Desmond at a nightclub back when Steve was doing very well as a headhunter. Steve knew the nightclub Desmond worked at was the kind of nightclub that was frequented by the types of people who engaged in alternative lines of work, including the kind of work that could help Steve with his concern.

So when Steve asked Desmond if any of the regulars at the night club might be interested in working with him on his "project," Desmond immediately thought of the two men, who he presumed to be brothers, even though he wasn't sure if they were brothers and even though he wasn't sure what they did exactly.

As it turned out, the two men were indeed interested in meeting Steve. And because of that, they were now gym members and they were now smoking again.

"Gimme a carton of those cigarettes that can be both regular cigarettes and menthols," the older brother said to the owner of the liquor store. "And a lighter. A red one."

"You get five cents off your lighter when you buy a carton of cigarettes," said the owner.

"Oh boy!" said the younger brother in a facetious manner. "Now that's what I call a deal."

The owner would normally have said something back to the customer in this situation. He would have shot his mouth off real good. But he'd been sizing up the two men since they'd entered the store and they seemed to him the kind of men where if you said something to them that they took the wrong way, it might not end well for you.

So instead he just looked as agitated as possible as he handed the older brother his change and didn't say anything more.

The brothers stepped outside, tore into the carton of cigarettes, and lit up. There was a sign on the front of the liquor store that read NO SMOKING WITHIN 20 FEET OF BUILDING. But the brothers ignored it. Or maybe they didn't see it. But either way, they were smoking where they technically shouldn't have been smoking. The owner wasn't about to tell them to go smoke elsewhere, but Lenny had no trouble telling the two men to beat it.

"Hey!" said Lenny. "You can't smoke there! Go do it somewhere else!"

Lenny was sitting in a wingback chair on the sidewalk. The owner of the liquor store allowed Lenny to sell incense in front of the liquor store every Friday. The owner didn't ask for a cut of Lenny's sales; he just felt bad for Lenny and allowed him to sell his incense one day a week in front of his establishment.

Lenny was probably around seventy. It was hard to tell how old he was exactly, because he was homeless and he didn't groom himself. He had thinning, sandy blonde hair and a wispy sandy blonde beard. His face was always sunburned because he sat out in the sun all day and never put on sunscreen. Ironically, Lenny could have afforded sunscreen if he wanted to, because even though he was homeless, he always made a decent profit from selling incense. But he chose to spend his money on other things like liquor and canned tuna and lottery tickets.

Lenny hadn't always been homeless and he hadn't always been unkempt. When he was younger, people regularly told him he resembled an attractive version of Jimmy Carter. But no one told him that anymore. Most people he came into contact with these days didn't even know who Jimmy Carter was.

The other homeless people in the neighborhood considered

Lenny to be a mogul of sorts because of his incense business. In their eyes, he was very well off. Lenny kept the money from his incense sales in a coffee tin and he also carried a knife in case it ever occurred to the other homeless people that they could try to rob him and take his money.

Lenny didn't like people asking him who supplied him with his incense. That was one of his pet peeves. One time a fellow homeless person named Charlie innocently asked Lenny where he got his incense from, and without saying a word, Lenny took out his knife and stabbed him right in the leg.

Charlie never again asked Lenny where he got his incense from because Charlie had no desire to get stabbed again.

Unlike the owner of the liquor store, Lenny was not good at sizing up people. That was one of the reasons Lenny was homeless. Because he couldn't size up people and make good decisions when it came to interacting with others, it was difficult for him to get a job.

And now here he was not doing a good job of sizing up the two men as he shot off his mouth real good.

"Are you deaf? The sign says NO SMOKING! Get lost, you animals!"

The two brothers might have been killers, but they weren't completely humorless. So they just smiled at Lenny as they continued to smoke where they technically shouldn't have been smoking.

Lenny wasn't used to people not moving when he told them they shouldn't be smoking where the two men were currently smoking. Usually people moved right away because they didn't want to continue getting yelled at by a strange, elderly homeless person who was sitting in a wingback chair on the sidewalk.

But these two men were different. They clearly weren't getting it. So Lenny had no choice but to stand up and waddle over to them and really give them what for. "Listen, you S.O.B.s, I'm gonna give you exactly three seconds to move it along, or else, well, it ain't gonna be pretty."

Now Lenny was really starting to irritate the two brothers. When they made the decision to start smoking again for the first time in twelve years, they did it partly in the hopes of meeting attractive women who would want to bum cigarettes off them after a vigorous, ass-kicking workout at the gym. They didn't have any interest in meeting homeless people like Lenny.

Lenny was more than a little off his rocker, but he was also a man of his word, and now that three seconds had passed and the two men hadn't moved, he pulled out his knife and attempted to stab the older brother in the leg.

Before Lenny could complete his stab, however, the younger brother knocked the knife out of Lenny's hand.

Their adrenaline was really racing at this point as the two men grabbed Lenny and rushed him into the alley next to the liquor store. They threw him against a wall and the older brother punched Lenny in the face. Then the younger brother punched Lenny in the stomach. Then the older brother took his head, bashed it into the wall, and watched an unconscious Lenny fall to the ground.

Under normal circumstances, that probably would have been the end of Lenny's beating. Unfortunately for Lenny, however, the younger brother spotted a cinder block lying next to a dumpster, so he walked over and picked it up, then he walked back to Lenny and brought it down on Lenny's head with as much force as he could muster.

And then Lenny was dead. The two brothers knew immediately that he was dead because they were in the killing business and one of their job requirements was to be able to immediately identify when someone was dead.

So they picked up Lenny's newly deceased body and tossed it into the nearby dumpster. Then they collected themselves, pocketed Lenny's knife, and went back around the corner to retrieve the carton of cigarettes the older brother had dropped when they'd grabbed Lenny and forced him into the alley. Then they went on their way.

The liquor store owner didn't see any of this. He didn't hear anything, either. The liquor store owner was too busy hating his life.

38

Steve was sitting in a diner with his father, but he was distracted. He could only think about where Kelly went when she'd left the house earlier in the day.

Steve was almost certain that Kelly wouldn't go to the police. What good would that do? Sure, he and Kelly hadn't been getting along lately, but that didn't necessarily mean she'd just throw her husband under the bus as soon as she got some dirt on him.

Besides, Steve hadn't actually *done* anything yet. No one had officially been killed as far as he knew. Sure, he'd given the two men some money, but if anyone ever pressed him on it, he could just say it was a loan. People lent money to people all the time, so why would this situation raise an eyebrow?

Plus, wouldn't Kelly be putting her own reputation on the line by going to the police? Worst case scenario, say the police believed her and then the story got leaked to the press and then Steve got arrested—is that something Kelly would really want? Then she'd just get dragged through the mud along with Steve. She'd forever be known as the wife of the guy who attempted to have a gym manager killed.

Steve didn't know if Kelly was much into legacies, but he was fairly certain she would definitely not want *that* to be her legacy.

So Steve was pretty sure he was fine. Maybe she really had just gone to get some fresh air. That's what his father said she'd done. And when Steve and his father had left to go to the diner, her car was still at the house. So yes, that was probably all she was doing was getting some fresh air—unless of course, she'd walked to the police station. *But who the hell walks to a police station?*

No one. That's who. No one walks to police stations, regardless of how angry they might be at their spouse, and regardless of what kind of dirt they might have on someone.

People simply did not walk to police stations. They drove.

Thinking about how people never walked to police stations momentarily put Steve's mind at ease. But that ease quickly evaporated as he realized he couldn't possibly know for sure where Kelly was or what she might be thinking unless he spoke to her. So he excused himself from the table and went outside to call her.

Steve's father was drinking an iced tea, and he was nervous doing even that. He couldn't remember the last time he'd stepped foot in a diner. It must have been when he was a boy. He recalled how his parents had nothing against diners. They would occasionally eat at them, he knew. It wasn't until Steve's father was working on his doctorate that he fully began to realize the importance of eating food made with love and how difficult it could be to find that type of food outside the home.

He'd done his best with Steve. It wasn't easy being a single parent, and it wasn't easy being a pharmacist. He'd done everything in his power to show his son the merits of not wearing a baseball glove and not eating in diners, but he also knew you can't control your children's choices once they become adults, and if Steve was going to wear baseball gloves and eat at diners, there was nothing he could do to stop it.

"More iced tea?" said the waitress as she set a heaping pile of pancakes down at Steve's place.

Steve's father looked at his iced tea. He'd barely touched it. What on earth was this waitress thinking? How could he possibly want more iced tea when his glass was already full? Was there something in the tea? Was that what got people addicted to diners?

He knew he should have simply ordered a glass of water or nothing at all. Good God, why had he agreed to join his son at a diner?

Before Steve's father could answer, Steve returned to his seat. He had not been able to get a hold of Kelly. He left a message for her to call him and said nothing more than that.

The last thing he needed was to accidentally incriminate himself in a voicemail. He had to be smart. He had to play things close to the vest. Going forward, no one else could know his plan.

Steve looked down at his pancakes and realized he wanted nothing to do with them. His worrying about Kelly had caused him to lose his appetite. But he knew he'd better eat them as he didn't want his father to think anything was amiss. Steve hadn't let the two men get to him earlier in the morning, and he wasn't going to let his father get to him, either. This was a new Steve: a more controlled Steve.

"Could I get some extra syrup?" Steve asked the waitress. There. That would do it. Now Steve's father would have no idea about the inner hell Steve currently found himself trapped in. Steve had just ordered extra syrup, so clearly everything was just fine in Steve's world. Everything was hunky motherfucking dory.

Steve's father was also playing things close to the vest. Even though the waitress was potentially trying to poison him with hate-filled iced tea or whatever illegal substances they put in diner food, he wasn't for one second going to let his son know that he was out of his element. He was going to sit there calmly and ignore the rage that was growing in his stomach. When it came to diners, Steve's father had the same reaction Steve had when Steve would see little wooden boats. He'd see red. He'd go ballistic. He'd fly off the handle.

But not today. No, sir. No way, Jose.

Steve cut into his pancakes, taking a huge bite he didn't really want to take. "Since you haven't told me yet, and you're clearly going to make me ask, do you mind telling me what you're doing here?"

"Steve, I have some bad news."

Christ, thought Steve. *Alzheimer's*. It had to be Alzheimer's. It ran on his father's side of the family. It had gotten the two Scotties, and now it had gotten his father.

Steve might have detested his old man, but he wasn't going to not feel bad for him in this moment, either.

"Alzheimer's?" said Steve.

Steve's father was confused. "Alzheimer's? What about Alzheimer's?"

Now Steve was confused. "You know, *Alzheimer's*. You have Alzheimer's."

"Alzheimer's? No, I don't have Alzheimer's. I'm a pharmacist. Do you really think I would spend my whole life working as a pharmacist only to develop Alzheimer's? I swore an oath never to get sick, and by God I'm going to honor that oath."

"Shit, sorry I said anything at all," said Steve.

"No," said Steve's father. "The tree is sick. The oak tree in our yard. The one I moved from your grandparents' home after your mother died. It has Oak wilt, which is similar to Dutch elm disease. Steve, the tree has to come down and I wanted to make sure you knew, because I know how much that tree means to you. Hell, I know how much that tree means to *me*."

Steve was speechless. He'd never thought that tree could possibly die. It was a mighty oak after all. Plus, it had survived being uprooted and replanted in their backyard. Very few trees could have lived through that trauma without suffering transplant shock. No, this tree was meant to live!

And since he'd treated that tree as if it was the reincarnation of his mother all these years, he felt in a way that he was now losing his mother for a second time. There was no way he was going to be able to force himself to eat his pancakes now. This was sad news for both him and his father as they both had a horse in this race. It was probably the only race the two of them had ever had horses in together.

"I don't know what to say," said Steve, setting down his fork.

For the first time in a long time, Steve's father felt like he could

152

be a father again to Steve. He would help guide his son through this. In fact, he'd already started that process. "I want you to come home. I want you to come home and I want you to be the one who chops down the tree."

"What? You can't just..."

Steve's father cut him off. "I know, I know, it sounds strange. But I've already made the arrangements. I have a friend who works for the city and he owed me a favor, and it's okay. There's no red tape.

"I... this... this is a lot," said Steve, letting out a huge exhale.

"Steve, would you think about it? Would you at least think about it? This could be good for you. You've done a lot of quitting in your life. You quit the baseball team, you quit being a lumberjack, but now you have an opportunity to..."

"Hey! I did not *quit* being a lumberjack. I was forced out, damnit! There's a huge difference!"

A moment ago, when Steve thought his father might have developed Alzheimer's, he'd actually started empathizing with his dad. When had he ever done that before? But now Steve's father was using the death of his symbolic mother to let Steve know what he really thought about him, and it was now painfully obvious that he thought of his son as being a quitter and just like that, all the anger Steve had harbored toward his father over the years came rushing back.

And now Steve found himself telling his father the same thing he'd told him when he was fourteen years old: "But either way, I'd still rather be known as a quitter than be known as a spitter!"

Before Steve's father could counter, the waitress returned to drop off the syrup Steve had no intention of using. Then she set down a full glass of iced tea in front of Steve's father that Steve's father had no intention of drinking.

"Just in case you change your mind," she said with a wink.

39

Chester sat at his desk, rubbing sanitizer on his hands.

He'd just finished his fourth cigarette of the day. Or was it his fifth? Shoot, it was going to be one of those days. Usually Chester limited himself to smoking three to five cigarettes a day when he was at the gym, but he was already close to maxing that out and there was still plenty of day left.

Oh, well. Every day was different. And if today his body needed more cigarettes than normal, so be it.

He hadn't looked closely at the two men's IDs when he'd made photocopies of them earlier in the day, but as he now processed their paperwork, he couldn't help but notice that neither man was fifty-two.

Based on the information on their IDs, one of them was forty-nine, and the other one was fifty-five. They both had the same last name—Thompson—but neither was fifty-two.

Why would someone claim to be fifty-two who wasn't? thought Chester.

The two men definitely were peculiar; there was no getting around that. And if he was being completely honest, Chester wasn't sure that having them as members would enhance the gym's character.

At the same time, membership was down. It was down quite a bit, in fact. And Chester knew that if the numbers continued to sag, he might very well be out of a job at some point.

So Chester decided it was worth the risk. Although they were gruff at first (and overly concerned about urine in the pool), the two men definitely seemed to be excited to join the gym. And Chester also knew that after a month or two, that excitement would most likely wear off, and then the men would start coming to the gym less frequently, until they most likely wouldn't come at all. And after a year, when their memberships were up, they probably wouldn't renew them, and then Chester would never see them again.

It was coming up on the time of day when Chester would normally make his rounds and make sure every part of the gym was running smoothly. But Chester didn't feel like making his rounds. He felt like smoking another cigarette.

He stepped outside to discover his pack was empty. He thought for sure he had a couple left, but then he remembered he'd bummed some to the two men, and another to Daphne. So Chester walked to the liquor store to buy some more.

Chester had been buying cigarettes at the liquor store for a long time. He knew it was Friday and Lenny would be out front selling his incense, so Chester was a bit surprised to see Lenny's chair and incense outside the liquor store, but no sign of Lenny. But Chester didn't think too much of it. Lenny was peculiar after all, and Chester had already spent a good part of his day thinking about how the two men were peculiar, so the last thing he wanted to do was devote any more time to thinking about peculiar people. To hell with that.

The liquor store owner was happy to see Chester. Chester was one of the few people who could put a smile on his face.

"Greetings, Chester. What's new?"

"Not much, Hank. Just throwing my money away again."

"Well, you can throw your money away here anytime!"

Chester put some money on the counter and Hank gave Chester his cigarettes and his change.

"See ya, Hank."

"Take care, Chester."

Chester walked outside and opened his pack of cigarettes. Normally, he would have walked back to the gym to smoke there, but since Lenny wasn't around to tell him to go smoke somewhere else, Chester decided he'd smoke in front of the liquor store for a change.

And as he did, he didn't think another thought about Lenny.

40

Steve and his father didn't talk at all on the drive back to Steve's house. Steve's father was shaken from his experience at the diner and was worried he might have drunk iced tea made from hate and he wasn't sure how that might affect his body. He'd be sure to take some vitamins before he went to bed to ward off any potential illness.

So that was one of the reasons the two men didn't talk—because of Steve's father's diner paranoia.

Another reason they didn't talk was because when they left the diner Steve told his father he didn't want to talk to him in person anymore. He told his father that over the years he'd grown accustomed to communicating with him via letters, and that was how he wanted to continue to interact with him. He didn't want any more of this "in-person bullshit" as Steve had phrased it.

Steve's father told him he would accept that and he would wait to receive a letter from Steve letting him know whether or not he wanted to come back to chop down the oak tree. He told Steve to do his best to send him a letter sooner than later, though, since it was a time-sensitive situation.

Even though Steve was very interested in going back to the house he grew up in to chop down the oak tree, he wasn't about to let his father know that—at least not at that moment. Instead,

Steve told his father he was done talking to him, that he would drive him back to his house to get his rental car, and then Steve's father had better be on his way immediately and he'd better not even think about asking to use Steve's bathroom—that was out of the question. He was not going to be allowed back in Steve's house under any circumstances.

Once they arrived at Steve's house, Steve's father opened the door, got out, and did not say anything further to Steve.

Steve then drove away. Steve's father thought it odd that Steve didn't go back in his house, but then he thought maybe Steve had to be at work.

Steve's father got in his rental car and put the key in the ignition. He didn't start the car, though. He looked at Steve's house. It was an okay house, he thought. It wasn't a great house, but it was fine. He really had wanted the world for Steve. He wanted him to be someone special—someone who did great things and helped others.

Of course, Steve *was* special. It was just, maybe he could have been more special than he already was if he'd just... *Oh, what does it matter now*, Steve's father thought to himself.

At least his son was here. He was alive. And although Steve didn't seem to be particularly happy (and it was painfully obvious he was having marital problems), Steve's father couldn't recall a time when Steve had really *ever* been happy, except when he was talking to that oak.

Steve's father had never meant to eavesdrop on Steve, but when Steve was a boy, he did occasionally catch him talking to the oak tree, sharing things with the tree he never shared with his father.

And this morning, Steve's father had once again not intended to eavesdrop on his son, but he couldn't help but overhear Steve on the phone, talking to someone about eight hundred dollars and "making a drop." That sure had sounded suspicious, whatever it was. For a moment, he worried about Steve and hoped he wasn't involved in some type of sketchy situation. But then he recalled how independent Steve was, how he was always able to stand up for himself, and what a stubborn S.O.B. he was. So maybe that phone call was just Steve haggling over a plumbing bill, or maybe Steve was simply negotiating to buy a lawnmower. Didn't lawnmowers usually cost around eight hundred dollars?

He had to admit his surprise visit had not gone well. Perhaps he should have just written Steve a letter. But his concern was if he wrote Steve a letter, how would he know for sure that Steve received it? What if Steve never confirmed receipt? By dropping in on him, at least he'd been able to tell Steve in person about the dire state of the oak tree, and now the ball was firmly in Steve's court.

Steve's father knew Steve detested the tiny boats he made, and Steve had already rejected the two he'd brought for him and Kelly, but Kelly had seemed to take a liking to them, so Steve's father retrieved the boats from the trunk of his car and walked them up to Steve's house and left them on the doorstep. Maybe Kelly would get to them first and find a use for them.

And if Steve got to them first, well…

41

Eric and Kelly spent the day at the museum. They had a late lunch at the museum café and they capped the afternoon off with a walk around the museum's sculpture garden.

They both put on a complimenting clinic throughout the day, easily exceeding the ten daily compliments at which they were goaled. Steve complimented one of the museum security guards on the sweater she was wearing. Kelly told the server at the café to pass along to the chef that he'd made a killer Portobello mushroom sandwich. Steve complimented the woman running the museum bookstore on her colorful eyewear and sense of style. Kelly complimented another security guard on how great he was at being quiet. Even the parking attendant received a compliment for having a well-groomed mustache.

"We just had a date, didn't we?" said Eric as he and Kelly drove back to his house.

"I think so," Kelly laughed. "It's been so long since I've been on one that I can't really remember what they feel like, but I'm pretty sure that was a date."

Eric put his hand on Kelly's thigh and Kelly put her hand on Eric's hand. Whatever they were on, neither of them wanted it to end.

"I'd like to make us dinner," said Eric. "I can pick up some groceries on the way home. Would that work for you?"

"That works for me. Is there anything I can make? How about a salad?"

"Sure, you can make a salad."

"How do you feel about carrot salad?"

"I love carrot salad!"

Kelly squeezed Eric's hand. Finally, a man who appreciated carrot salad.

It was evening by the time Eric fired up the grill. He and Kelly were standing on his patio, both enjoying a glass of wine as they stared up at the sky.

"So, are you going to introduce me?" said Kelly.

"Introduce you?"

"To the star! To Cliff."

"Oh! Of course!"

Eric had completely forgotten he'd told Kelly about Cliff. He pointed at a house across the street. "Well, I honestly can't tell you which one he is for sure, but you see that house? If you start at the roof of the house and then look straight up to the first row of stars and then count five stars to the left, I'm pretty sure he's that fifth star."

Kelly did her best to follow the path Eric pointed out, but of course had no idea which star he was referring to exactly. But that wasn't going to prevent her from playing along: "He's gorgeous," she said.

Eric laughed. "You hear that, Cliff? She thinks you're gorgeous."

Kelly laughed, too. Then Eric shook his head with a smirk.

"What's wrong?"

"Nothing," said Eric. "It's just, you must think I'm insane for talking to a star. That's all."

Kelly did not think Eric was insane for talking to a star. Her husband talked to a tree, for God's sake. Kelly just assumed that's what men did. Men weren't always the best at communicating with other people, so that's why they liked to talk to inanimate objects like trees or stars or blowup dolls, because those kinds of things couldn't talk back to them and tell them they were bad listeners or that their ideas were for the birds.

She considered sharing with Eric how Steve talked to a tree throughout his childhood, but she and Eric were having such a great time—why risk ruining the moment by bringing up her husband?

She'd seen Steve's missed call and voicemail notification earlier in the day. She didn't listen to the voicemail and then turned her phone off in case he tried to call again. She didn't feel like talking about his stupid plan to have someone murdered. Sometimes Steve's dumb ideas really were for the birds.

He was most likely calling to tell her not to go to the police or something like that. Steve was always thinking about himself first. She was sure Steve wasn't calling to make sure she was okay; he was just calling to cover his own ass.

He hadn't always been so angry and bitter. For years, he'd been a model husband. But Kelly couldn't remember the last time he'd gone out of his way to do something nice for her. And even last night, when he wanted to take her out for dinner and champagne, that wasn't because he really wanted to spend time with her. It was because he wanted to celebrate someone's impending death.

Steve had really outdone himself this time. Talk about going off the deep end. There was only one thing left for Kelly to do now, and that was to get out.

And while there was never a perfect time to end a marriage, at least Kelly now had Eric, a man who definitely loved her—who had wolf love for her, even—and who had gone out of his way multiple times today to do nice things for her.

Additionally, Steve's father's fortuitous visit had given Kelly the idea that she could become a pharmacist. So perhaps it was true—perhaps the universe *did* provide, and when it took something away from you, it then gave you something else in its place.

Kelly was experiencing intense feelings of abundance flowing through her as she blurted out, "I think I'm going to become a pharmacist!"

That wasn't the response Eric had expected to hear when he told Kelly she must think him insane for talking to a star, but that also wasn't going to prevent him from being happy for her.

"That's great!" said Eric. Kelly's exhilaration about becoming a pharmacist had caught him a bit off guard, so he fumbled around for a moment to come up with a follow-up question, but eventually he got out, "Has that always been a dream of yours?"

"Not really," said Kelly. "Not until this morning. But I'm pretty sure that's what I want to do with my life." Kelly grabbed the bottle of wine from the table and refilled both of their glasses. "And I just know I'd be great at it—just like you're so great at giving and receiving compliments."

Kelly raised her glass to toast Eric, but Eric didn't lift his glass to meet hers.

"I'm not sure how to say this," said Eric, "but I'm going to be transitioning away from compliments. I've given it a lot of thought, and I do want to thank you for how supportive you've always been about my complimenting-giving abilities, but in the long run, I don't think it's what I want to be doing with my life."

This was certainly upsetting news for Kelly as throughout the day she'd been thinking that when she found the right moment, she would convince Eric to come back to the final compliments class so he could take the final exam and get his certificate. He'd come so far—so what if he'd missed one class recently? He still had time to study and could easily ace the exam. And if Eric wanted, she'd be more than happy to help him prepare for it.

Now it was looking like this was not going to happen and it was making Kelly more than a little sad.

"A couple days ago, I signed up for a finders class," said Eric. "Did you know we spend nearly three whole days out of the year just looking for things we've misplaced? Think about what we could do with that extra time!"

Despite her initial disappointment, Kelly couldn't help but be drawn in by Eric's newly found exuberance for finding things. Selfishly speaking, she wished he would continue his complimenting studies, but if he'd been bitten by the finders bug, so be it!

Kelly had just been bitten by the pharmacist bug herself, so who was she to judge?

"If it makes you happy," said Kelly, "then I support your decision one hundred percent."

Kelly put her arm around Eric and drew him in for a kiss.

"You ready for some salmon?" said Eric.

"I am," said Kelly. "Are you ready for some carrot salad?"

Eric smiled. "Born ready."

As Eric put the salmon on the grill, Kelly went into the kitchen to whip up a carrot salad. This might have been the first time Eric and Kelly had cooked dinner together, but that didn't prevent them from easily falling into a rhythm on par with the top kitchen brigades in the world.

And if stars were capable of feeling pride, Cliff would have been bursting with it.

42

Steve was washing the windshield of a brown Aspen. The Aspen belonged to a woman named Sylvia. Sylvia was one of the gas station's best customers. Even though Glen was fairly repellant-looking, she'd always had a crush on him and she would fill her tank at his gas station every week and flirt with him. That was Sylvia's social life—flirting with Glen. It wasn't much of a social life, but Sylvia was older and not looking for a relationship at that point of her life, so flirting with Glen once a week was all she needed. Sylvia knitted, too. And one time she made Glen an afghan. Glen wasn't sure what to make of it—but he thanked her for it, and then used it to dust the counters at the gas station. He still had the afghan, and he still used it to dust the counters.

Now that Steve was working for him, Glen would send Steve out to tend to Sylvia whenever she pulled into the station. Glen didn't dislike Sylvia, but now that he had the option of not having to deal with her, he took advantage of that opportunity.

The first couple of times Steve filled Sylvia's tank and washed her windshield and checked her tire pressure and checked her oil, Sylvia would ask where Glen was and who Steve was and all those other questions that people ask when they've been accustomed to working with one person and then all of a sudden that person is gone and now they have to work with another person that they don't know at all and they're concerned the new person might not be as good at doing things as the previous person and they're reminded of the impermanence of life and that frightens them a bit.

Eventually, though, Sylvia stopped asking about Glen entirely and would instead flirt with Steve. She had to admit, Steve was certainly better-looking than Glen and he was nicer than Glen and he smiled more than Glen and he definitely smelled better than Glen. And when Sylvia eventually made an afghan for Steve, he immediately knew what it was and thanked her for it. He didn't have a puzzled look on his face like Glen had when she'd given Glen his afghan.

"Okay, Sylvia. Everything's looking good. It's going to be ten twenty-four."

Sylvia handed Steve a twenty. "Thank you for taking such good care of my baby, Steve."

"I'll get you some change. Be right back."

This was Sylvia's favorite part of fueling up at the gas station, because this was the part where she got to check out Steve's butt. She loved to watch Steve and his butt walk away from her car and disappear into the store. She knew Steve was married, but she also knew it wasn't a crime to have a look every now and then. Some butts were made to be looked at, and as far as Sylvia was concerned, Steve's butt was one of them.

Sylvia primped her hair in the rearview mirror and reapplied her lipstick as Steve returned with her change. She took the change and handed Steve a dollar. She always tipped Steve a dollar.

"And that's for you," she said.

"Thanks, Sylvia."

"You know, Steve, when those new gas stations open up, I don't care if they *give* the gas away, I'm staying loyal to you and Glen. You're never going to lose my business!"

Steve smiled. "We appreciate that, Sylvia. Thank you."

"Yes, sir," said Sylvia. "You have a good weekend now. Make sure you have some fun!"

166

Sylvia gave Steve a sly smile as she drove off.

Steve liked Sylvia. He liked everything about working at the gas station. He liked that Glen basically let him run the place. He also liked that he hadn't been required to do administrative work for years before he was allowed to take part in the action. He was thrown into the action immediately!

Lumberjack bonds ran deep, and that's why Glen trusted Steve so much. At least, that's what Steve told himself. He knew that part of the reason Glen had given Steve the run of the place was also because Glen was losing his mind. But Steve didn't dwell on that too much. He just focused on doing the best job he could do by keeping the gas station clean and keeping the supply of baseball cards well-stocked.

When Steve wasn't working at the gas station or sleeping at the gas station, he could be found drinking at the bar. Sometimes Glen would join him for a couple of beers and they'd share lumberjack stories. Steve would always feel a little embarrassed when he and Glen talked about being lumberjacks since Glen had been a lumberjack for seventeen years and Steve had only been a lumberjack for four days. But whenever Steve was hanging his head for having been a lumberjack for such a short period of time, Glen would always remind him that being a lumberjack for four days was something to be proud of and definitely not something to be ashamed of. "Hell," Glen would say, "you need to have cojones the size of the Empire State Building to even become a lumberjack in the first place!"

That would always cheer Steve up, anytime Glen reminded him he was a courageous person for having pursued a career as a lumberjack. Yes, maybe most of his time had been spent performing administrative tasks, but he'd also learned how to break up fights, a skill that would come in handy for the rest of his life. It was a skill he was also able to pass along to his wife.

Kelly had been hired by the bar to work as a bouncer. Kelly and Steve had been drinking at the bar one night and were shooting the breeze with Ernie, the bartender with the perfect teeth who was accustomed to receiving lousy tips.

They were talking about how Kelly was getting a little bored, now that Steve had a job and she didn't and they were in this town where there wasn't too terribly much to do and she was thinking she should get a job, because otherwise she was just spending most of her days in the car and that was starting to make her depressed.

"I'll talk to the owner," said Ernie. "Maybe we can make you a server! I have to tell you, the tips are pretty lousy, but…"

"No, thank you," said Kelly. "My serving days are behind me."

Ernie shrugged and was about to say he couldn't think of any other positions the bar could potentially offer Kelly, but he was interrupted by the sound of two quarreling women. One of the women had pinned the other woman to the ground and was belching loudly in her face.

"You think my breath stinks? Well what about NOW?" the woman on top yelled. Then she belched in the other woman's face some more. The woman who was pinned to the ground then spat at the woman who was on top because there wasn't much else she could do since her arms and legs were immobilized.

A few men had gathered and were cheering the two women on. They were waving money around and appeared to be placing bets as to which woman would win the fight.

Ernie jumped in to break up the fight, and then the two women unexpectedly joined forces and started attacking Ernie. One of the women bit his shoulder and the other woman scratched his cheek and his chest.

The men were really enjoying this and continued to pass money back and forth. It was hard to tell which person the men were betting on to win, but it was obvious they found this brawl very entertaining.

The women now had Ernie pinned to the ground and were belching in his face and doing other things to him that Ernie hadn't given them permission to do. That's when Steve stepped in and wedged himself between the women and Ernie with a precision that was so impressive that it stopped everything. It stopped the fight, it stopped the betting, and it even stopped the belching.

He then grabbed the women by the backs of their shirts and led them outside. When he re-entered the bar, he found Kelly tending to Ernie. He'd been scratched a few times, but he'd be okay. And thankfully his perfect teeth were still perfect.

"I like most things about my job," said Ernie, "but I can't stand it when the customers fight. I was not put on this earth to deal with this crap."

"Maybe you need a bouncer," said Steve.

"I'd love that," said Ernie. "But I'd have to ask the owner and I don't know what we could pay you."

"Not me," said Steve. "Kelly."

Kelly's eyes lit up. Of course! Why hadn't she thought of that herself? She remembered the night at the diner when she and Steve first met—how deftly he'd defused that fight and how he'd done it when he could barely walk!

If Steve spent some time training her and taught her everything he knew, she was sure she could have great success as a bouncer. It would also give her something to do and she could make some money that she and Steve could put toward a down payment on a house, and that would get them out of the car quicker.

"I'll teach her everything I know," said Steve. "I'm an expert at breaking up fights."

Ernie seemed hesitant.

"And if for some reason things get out of hand, just call over to the gas station and I'll come running. It's a win-win."

Kelly nodded. "I can do it, Ernie. I won't let you down."

Ernie was still a bit dazed from what had just transpired, but this also wasn't the craziest thing he'd ever heard. With Steve's guidance, maybe Kelly would work out just fine. And when he thought about it, it really was the women that tended to get out of hand at the bar. Ernie never understood why that was. The men would get drunk, and occasionally disorderly, but they wouldn't get into actual fights that needed to be broken up. It was the women who fought. And Ernie was sick and tired of having to step in

169

between them. So if Kelly wanted that duty, it was all hers. He'd have to clear it with the owner, but he was confident they could work something out.

In the coming years, Steve would go on to place numerous bouncers at numerous jobs, but it was the placement of his wife that he always found to be the most rewarding. And the fact that he didn't accept a bribe to make it happen made it all the sweeter.

43

The events of the past few days, culminating in the arrival of Steve's father with the news of the dying oak tree, had put Steve in a mood he wasn't used to experiencing. That mood was a reflective mood.

When he was growing up, he would reflect on a regular basis since he had the oak tree to talk to. But once he left home to become a lumberjack, he never looked back. Sure, he'd made some poor decisions, like everyone does from time to time, but he always kept moving forward. He didn't stop to question things.

Even as his marriage was falling apart, he didn't think too deeply about it. He knew he and Kelly hadn't gotten along well for years now, but sometimes marriages just ended. In fact, marriages ended all the time—why should theirs be any different?

He and Kelly had grown sick of each other. It wasn't uncommon. Put two people together in close quarters and then have life with all of its unpredictabilities tug at them and toss them around for a few decades, and what do you get? Two disgruntled people who can barely stand the sight of each other.

Maybe they should have had kids. At least then they would have had something to show for their marriage. Maybe that would have given them both something to focus on instead of the emptiness of their own lives. The topic had come up several times over the years, but neither of them was ever particularly excited about it, so it just never happened. They both felt that in order to bring a new life into the world, what was required most was enthusiasm. Neither possessed that level of enthusiasm for raising a child, and an unplanned pregnancy never presented itself either, so they remained childless, and neither lost any sleep over it.

Kelly never worked all that much. She'd taken on part-time jobs here and there, but she never stuck with any of them for any length of time. Steve always made okay money, but it wasn't pharmacist money, so they never lived high off the hog.

Over the years, neither Steve nor Kelly was particularly interested in keeping up with the Joneses, so Kelly never pressured Steve to earn more money so they could buy a bigger house or join a country club, and Steve never bothered Kelly about staying home all the time. At least she kept the house in good shape, plus Steve liked playing the role of provider.

Steve knew he wasn't all that easy to live with. He was moody, he made snide remarks on a regular basis, and he wasn't open to new ideas like eating carrot salad. Sometimes he'd hit on women, too, but it never went any further than that, and he never did it when Kelly was around.

Losing his job a month ago had definitely been a blow, but he'd lost jobs before. And unlike when he lost his job as a lumberjack, this time around he didn't have to deal with getting his ass kicked by an army of former coworkers.

He hadn't told Kelly about losing his job because he didn't want her to worry. But more than that, he didn't want her to think he was a bigger loser than she already thought he was. He knew Kelly had once had the opportunity to marry a business major, and from time to time she would rub that in his face. She would always apologize after bringing it up, and Steve always pretended like it never bothered him all that much, but it did. At times like that, Steve always felt very much like a pine rider.

And he was currently feeling like a pine rider as he sat in his car in the parking lot of the Mexican restaurant by the freeway. The restaurant was where the gas station Steve worked at used to be. After the gas station was sold, it was converted into a Chinese restaurant, which had lasted a few years. Then it became a Thai restaurant, and that had been around for about seven years. Then it was briefly a pizza place, but the owner of the pizza place shot himself one night for reasons no one ever knew (although it was speculated that his business was going under, since other restaurants had failed in that same location), and now it was a Mexican restaurant. It was one of those restaurants that wasn't really a fast food restaurant and it wasn't really a sit-down place, either. It was one of those restaurants that confused Steve because he never knew if he was expected to dine in or take the food to go. As a result, Steve never went inside the restaurant.

He didn't go inside the restaurant today, either. Not even to use the restroom. He just sat in his car for hours and watched people go in and out. Judging by the lack of people going in and out, Steve wondered how much longer the Mexican restaurant would last, and what might take its place if it didn't survive. Maybe a donut shop. Steve had always thought a donut shop would do quite well in that spot.

Maybe this hadn't been the best time to hire the two men to knock off the Pool Pisser. Maybe he would have been better off using his money to invest in a donut shop or maybe he should have just looked for another job. Lately he'd had too much free time on his hands, and... damn, he forgot to bring his cologne. He was really feeling the need to splash some cologne on his face. Then he could think again. Why the hell did his father have to show up today of all days? Why did his beloved oak tree have to be suffering from a terminal illness? Weren't trees supposed to live for two hundred years or thereabouts? And where had Kelly gone?

He considered driving home, but if Kelly had gone to the police, the police would certainly be waiting for him. He also briefly thought about going on the lam, but that lifestyle didn't appeal to him. Instead, he grabbed his wallet and pulled out the picture of the oak tree. The photo had been through a lot over the years, and for someone looking at the photo for the first time, they probably wouldn't have known it was a tree they were looking at. The picture was that tattered.

But Steve knew it was a tree, and even though he hadn't spoken to the tree or the photo of the tree in forever, he felt the need to talk to it now.

"Mom," said Steve, "I think I might have screwed up. I think I might have really screwed the pooch this time."

He propped the photo up on his dashboard and stared at it. Usually when he spoke to his mother in this fashion, it would relax him. But this time it didn't seem to be working.

Steve was definitely in a place where he could have used a support group. But he had always been a lone wolf, and he'd grown increasingly bitter over the years since certain things in his life hadn't gone the way he'd hoped they would have gone. As a result, he didn't trust life all that much, and since he didn't trust life, that also made it difficult for him to trust other people. He and Chester had had a decent friendship for a while, but that friendship had obviously seen better days since he was now actively trying to kill Chester.

How had it come to this? Why hadn't he tried to build up the town's secret lumberjack society? Why had he let it fall by the wayside? Of course it wouldn't have been easy, but if he'd put just a little bit of effort into it, today he might have a group of former lumberjacks he could call upon to help him through whatever it was he was currently going through.

As he reflected on this, a woman with three kids started walking toward his car. Steve recognized the woman. Earlier, he'd noticed her and her children eating inside the restaurant. For a moment, Steve thought she was going to walk right up to his car. Then he realized she'd parked nearby. The woman had a scowl on her face and it was directed at Steve. It was one of those scowls that was very easy to interpret: the woman wanted to convey that she thought Steve was either a predator or a pervert or both, and she wanted to make sure he knew it.

Steve was taken aback that this woman had directed this scowl at him. Sure, he'd been looking at her and her kids a little bit while he was lost in thought, but he hadn't been looking at them like *that*. Good God, just the other day the two men had told him he looked dead and now this woman was giving him the pervert scowl. Was this really how people saw him?

Her point made, the woman got in her car with her children and drove off. If it had been another time, or even just a day ago when Steve was feeling more confident about his life direction, he would have told the woman to get lost and to stop silently accusing him of being a perv. Then he might have hit on her just to make the situation as uncomfortable as possible.

But where had that type of behavior gotten him? It had landed him at the parking lot of the Mexican restaurant—the very same parking lot he used to sleep at with Kelly when the parking lot had belonged to the gas station.

It was getting dark. Steve was emotionally drained and had given up on taking any further action for the day. So he closed his eyes and prayed he wouldn't have the baleen whale dream again.

44

Fortunately for Steve, he didn't have the baleen whale dream again. But Kelly did.

It was the first time she'd ever dreamed she was a baleen whale. She dreamed that she was at her wedding with Steve and the David Lee Roth impersonator. At first, Kelly was just Kelly. But after the David Lee Roth impersonator pronounced them man and wife, he threw confetti in the air and then Kelly turned into a baleen whale.

No one seemed to notice that she'd transformed into a whale. Steve kissed her and acted as if nothing was different. The David Lee Roth impersonator was also oblivious to her conversion. He just gave both Steve and Kelly a hug and then invited them back to his place for a threesome.

Steve said that sounded like a great idea. Kelly tried to protest, but she was a whale now so she couldn't speak. And no one was bothered by the fact that she was a whale! It was incredibly aggravating and was giving her a tremendous amount of anxiety. She was in no mood for a threesome. For God's sake, she'd just gotten married!

Kelly woke with a start to find Eric sleeping next to her. She'd spent the night. They'd had a lovely dinner and consumed copious amounts of wine. As they were drinking, Kelly knew Eric would be hungover the next day, just as she knew she would not be hungover. And sure enough, here she was wide awake at the crack of dawn, while Eric snored loudly next to her. She knew he was in for a long day—it would take him a while to recover.

She also found herself craving ketchup. She remembered Steve would occasionally complain about dreaming that he was a baleen whale and how he would crave ketchup afterwards. She'd always thought he was exaggerating, but now that she was experiencing it herself, she understood just how disorienting those experiences must have been for him and she wished she'd made more of an effort to be there for him during those times.

She turned her phone back on. It was 6:09 a.m. There weren't any more missed calls from Steve. She got dressed and felt compelled to go home immediately. She didn't know whether Steve would be waiting for her in a rage or whether he'd be hurt or whether she'd come home to find him completely indifferent to the fact she'd run off and not come home last night. All she knew was she had to go home.

As she got dressed, she started to feel guilty. She hadn't felt guilty at all yesterday when she was sleeping with Eric and complimenting people at the museum with him and cooking with him. But now she couldn't help but feel bad that she hadn't been faithful to Steve. He might have become a real jerk over the years, but he was still her husband, and when they got married she'd promised to stay with him through thick and thin and through life's ups and downs and whatever else it was that people said at weddings.

Just a few days ago she was worried about his health and offering him carrot salad, and now she was sleeping with one of her classmates behind his back. She and Eric had had quite a bit of sex, too. And the only thing that prevented them from having even more sex after dinner was that they were both pushing fifty and neither of them had had that much sex in a long, long time and they were both sore and worn out. So during and after dinner they'd just drunk themselves into oblivion instead.

Kelly thought about waking Eric to let him know she was leaving, but she was fairly certain that if she did, he would plead with her to stay and then he might start crying if she left and she'd have to tell him how much he meant to her in order to calm him down and then he'd whine, *But when can I see you again?* and she wouldn't be able to give him a definitive answer and she really didn't want to see him in that state. They'd had a lovely day yesterday and she didn't want anything souring it so soon.

So Kelly went downstairs and spent some time cleaning the dishes they'd used last night. She also found some ketchup in Eric's refrigerator and squeezed a bit onto her finger and licked it off. That took care of the ketchup craving. Next, she'd have to deal with Steve.

And as she thought about Steve, she decided she didn't want to feel guilty about her day with Eric. She didn't want to say Steve was a hundred percent to blame for what had happened (Kelly of course shared a good amount of responsibility), but Steve's lack of affection in recent years would have driven anyone away.

She found a piece of paper and a pen and started to write Eric a note, but then she realized she didn't quite know what to say. She knew he'd figure it out; she left. And if he desperately wanted to get a hold of her, it's not like he didn't know where she lived.

So she crumpled up the paper, put it in her purse, took out her phone to request a ride, and seven minutes later she was on her way home to deal with her husband who was either angry or hurt or indifferent, and perhaps not even home at all.

Then it dawned on Kelly that her father-in-law might be there, too. She sighed. Well, even if he was, at least she could talk to him further about becoming a pharmacist. If things ended up not working out between her and Steve she'd need to support herself somehow.

45

The two men were in Steve and Kelly's bedroom. They'd looked Steve up in the phone book and that's how they'd found where he lived.

Shortly after they'd killed Lenny, it dawned on the younger brother that he'd told Chester his actual age, but then he'd given Chester a fake ID that showed a different age. He wasn't sure if Chester would notice or not, but he told his brother about it and his brother decided they'd better kick things into high gear just to be on the safe side.

The older brother wasn't mad at his younger brother for slipping up. They'd been in this line of work for a long time and it was very difficult to always be pretending to be other people. Anyone could make a mistake once in a while. They had several fake IDs, and because they'd enjoyed talking to Chester so much, the younger brother was distracted and had simply given him the wrong one.

They knew they might have to kill Chester now, not because Steve wanted them to, but because they didn't want to risk having Chester go to the cops. They didn't like the idea of killing Chester since they'd just bonded with him and he'd inspired them to start smoking again. Plus, they really did want to take advantage of everything the gym had to offer. But business was business and if

Chester had to go, so be it.

Before they potentially killed Chester, though, they decided it was best to first pay Steve a surprise visit and make sure he had all the money he'd promised them. They'd been burned a couple times in the past and they weren't going to let that happen again.

In their experience, they learned it was always best to surprise someone just before the crack of dawn. They found that was usually when people were at their groggiest.

When they'd arrived at the house, they found two wooden boats on the front steps. The younger brother picked them up and smiled at them. Ever since the men had met Chester they were smiling a lot more and enjoying life more. The older brother also couldn't help but smile upon the sight of the boats. What kind of sick fuck could resist smiling at wooden boats?

They didn't have to say anything to each other; it was obvious they were taking these boats with them.

When it came to breaking into a house, they'd found it was always best to first check the front door before attempting any number of other break-in methods. They both put on a pair of gloves and then the older brother pushed down on the latch.

Fortunately for them, Steve had made it very easy for them to break in. In his rush to shoo his father out of his house the day before, Steve had completely forgotten to lock the front door.

So the men let themselves in. They crept around the first floor and found no one. Then they went upstairs and as quietly as possible ducked their head into each room as they gently walked down the hallway. Eventually they made it to the master bedroom.

The older brother took out the knife he'd taken from Lenny. It really was a good knife. He and his brother had been impressed that a homeless person would own such a good knife. It clearly had cost Lenny a pretty penny. That incense business Lenny was engaged in must have been fairly lucrative.

As they entered the bedroom, they quickly discovered there was no one there. They were sure that at least one person was going to be home since there was a car in the driveway, but maybe

Steve had left town? That wasn't uncommon, either. Sometimes in their line of work when a regular person wanted someone killed, they'd get cold feet and disappear. Maybe that's what had happened with Steve.

Still, they were in Steve's house now, and since Steve wasn't there to tell them where he kept his money, they might as well ransack the place and see if they couldn't find it themselves.

The men were excellent ransackers and it took them less than an hour to go through the whole house. They were very tidy ransackers, too, so after they ransacked a place, most of the time people didn't know they'd been ransacked at all. The brothers had oftentimes thought about how if ransacking wasn't so frowned upon in polite society, they could have taught ransacking courses all over the world and made a bundle. It truly was an art—an art they excelled at.

The last room they ransacked was the kitchen. After accepting the fact that the money wasn't anywhere in the house, they sat down at the kitchen table to catch their breath.

"I bet he's keeping it in the car," said the older brother.

"Yeah," said the younger brother, "I guess an idiot like that would."

"Well, he's gotta come home eventually."

"That he does."

The younger brother smiled at the boats he'd set on the kitchen table when they'd first entered the house. He picked one of them up to admire it more closely. Whoever made these boats was clearly an ace craftsman.

The older brother watched his younger brother inspect the boats for a moment, then turned his attention to the backyard and snorted loudly.

"What?" said the younger brother.

"I was just thinking," said the older brother, "they've got plenty of room for a pool!"

The younger brother smacked the kitchen table and let out a roar as the two men shared a laugh. They hadn't had this much fun working since, well, since *ever*.

The older brother wiped a tear from his eye as their laughter subsided. All that ransacking and laughing had made him thirsty. He got up to see what was in the refrigerator, and that's when they heard the sound of the front door opening as Kelly entered the house.

46

After a year, Steve and Kelly had saved up enough money to be able to move out of Kelly's car and into a house. Back then, the houses in their suburb were quite affordable since not many people wanted to live there yet. Steve and Kelly were happy with their new home and on occasion, they'd have Glen over for dinner.

This was back when Steve would still eat anything Kelly prepared and never complained about her cooking. Glen was always happy to join them since he didn't have much in the way of family, except for one son who lived far away and never visited Glen or checked in with Glen to see how he was doing. His son never once wrote him a letter.

Kelly liked cooking for Glen because he didn't drink to excess like her mother did and he never complained if Kelly served him a salad. Glen might not have been handsome, what with his brown teeth and his eye patch, and his unkempt hair, and his uneven eyes, but he did have a charm about him and Kelly always enjoyed his company.

On this particular evening, Glen joined them for dinner because he wanted to let Steve know that he was redrafting his will so that when he passed, the gas station would be left to Steve. He knew Steve would take great care of the gas station and would find a way to keep it afloat even though the new gas stations in town were already cutting into their business something fierce.

"Steve," said Glen between bites of chicken salad, "there's something important I want to talk to you about. And Kelly, I'm glad you're here, because I want you to hear this, too."

"We're all ears," said Steve.

Glen took a sip of milk and then went back to eating his dinner. He didn't mention the will. He'd already forgotten that he was going to talk to Steve and Kelly about it. Glen was losing his mind and there wasn't anything anyone could do about it.

This type of behavior was not uncommon for Glen, so Steve and Kelly did not prompt Glen to continue. They'd seen him do this many, many times before. He'd start talking about something and then he'd abruptly switch to a different topic or he'd just stop speaking altogether.

But on occasion, his brain would kick in and he'd remember what he was going to say. And this happened to be one of those occasions.

"Oh, right," said Glen, "the thing I was going to talk to you about. Steve, I would very much like for you to take over the gas station when I'm gone."

Steve grinned. "Where you going, Glen? Gonna take a cruise?" Steve occasionally liked to joke with Glen about taking a cruise. For whatever reason, the thought of Glen on a cruise always made Steve laugh. Steve just couldn't picture Glen mingling with other cruise-goers, or sunning himself, or playing shuffleboard. No matter how you sliced it, Glen just wasn't the cruise type.

Glen didn't mind this occasional cruise-ribbing, so he gave a polite smile. "No, Steve. No cruise for me. But when I die, I want you to have the gas station."

Kelly reached over and gave Glen a hug. "Oh, Glen. That is so generous."

"Well, it just makes sense," said Glen. "It just makes sense."

"I don't know what to say," said Steve.

"Don't have to say anything," said Glen.

Kelly squeezed Steve's hand under the table. Her life with

Steve was really taking off. She and Steve were both gainfully employed, they were the proud owners of a new house, and, not that she wanted to think about Glen dying or anything like that, but when nature did eventually take its course, she and Steve would own a gas station, so their retirement was basically taken care of. Everything was lining up and she was barely twenty years old!

Steve was blown away by Glen's generosity and was so happy that he and Kelly had decided to stop in this suburb and make it their home. He knew members of secret lumberjack societies were supposed to help one another out, but inheriting a gas station? That exceeded his wildest dreams.

Steve excused himself from the table and returned with three bottles of beer.

"I believe this calls for a toast," said Steve as he opened the bottles and passed them around. "To Glen, one of the greatest lumberjacks I've ever met, and more importantly, one of the greatest people I've ever met. I don't know what Kelly and I did to deserve you, but we can't thank you enough. Here's to Glen."

"To Glen," said Kelly.

They clanked their bottles and then everyone took a swig. Steve thought about how Glen had been more of a father to him than his actual father had been. Glen trusted Steve and let him run the gas station. His actual father never would have given him that much responsibility.

Kelly thought about how now maybe she could quit her job as the bouncer at the bar. The agreement she and Steve had made with the owner was that Kelly would receive a cut of the tips. Since Ernie was accustomed to accepting lousy tips, the money Kelly took home wasn't all that great. She tried to get Ernie to not accept lousy tips and to glare at customers when they left them, or serve customers slower when they left lousy tips, or not serve them at all.

She did her best to work with Ernie and try to change his psychology; she would tell him to repeat in his mind over and over, "I deserve substantial tips. I deserve substantial tips. I deserve substantial tips." But Ernie told Kelly that repeating that in his mind over and over just gave him a headache, and it also made him uncomfortable to not be nice to customers and to not laugh at their jokes, even if they didn't tip well.

It didn't matter what Kelly tried—whatever she did, nothing could change Ernie's mind. The tips remained lousy and so did Kelly's income. At least there had only been one fight since Kelly started working at the bar. Once word got out that the bar employed a bouncer, people started to behave better. Kelly wasn't particularly intimidating-looking. In fact, she wasn't intimidating-looking at all. But that just made people even more scared of her. People would wonder why on earth the bar would hire this petite woman as a bouncer if she wasn't some kind of fighting machine beneath the surface. No one dared test her, either, regardless of how drunk they got.

The only fight that happened when Kelly worked at the bar was when a married woman walked in to find her husband chatting with another woman. The wife started smacking the other woman with her purse, then the husband stepped in, pointed to Kelly, and said, "That's the bouncer! Don't let her see!"

Puzzled by Kelly's slight build, the wife was fairly certain she could kick Kelly's ass with both hands tied behind her back, but like all the other bar patrons, she didn't want to take the chance, because why else would this meek, young woman be the bouncer if she wasn't excellent at what she did?

So the wife simply told the other woman she'd smack her silly if she ever saw her again, and then she left.

Two weeks later, the wife ran into the other woman at the grocery store and stayed true to her word by smacking the woman silly over and over with a five-pound bag of flour. After that incident, some of the shoppers complained that the grocery store was no longer safe and they petitioned the manager to employ a bouncer.

A few of those irate shoppers went so far as to stand outside the grocery store and hound people to sign their petition that the grocery store needed to hire a bouncer to protect them from unforeseen attacks.

Ultimately, the shoppers were only able to obtain fourteen signatures, and six of those signatures were forged. There just weren't enough people who felt the grocery store needed a bouncer. The irate shoppers still presented the petition to the manager who smiled and told them that while he didn't know how many signatures they would have needed to obtain for the grocery store to make the change they were demanding, he was quite sure it would have taken a lot more than fourteen.

Instead, he handed each of the irate shoppers a coupon for a free can of tuna fish. The shoppers accepted the coupons and considered that to be a victory and then they went back out into the world to find other things to be irate about.

Glen had actually signed that petition, but if someone were to have told him that, he wouldn't have remembered doing it. He wasn't entirely sure what he was signing when he signed it. He thought perhaps it was for a chance to win a month's worth of free groceries. And who couldn't use a month's worth of free groceries?

But he'd forgotten that he'd signed it, just as he'd now forgotten he'd told Steve he was going to give him the gas station. Glen studied the bottle of beer in front of him. He didn't remember asking for a beer, but he was pretty sure it belonged to him.

"Mind if I drink this?" he said to Steve.

47

Steve awoke from a dreamless sleep. It was some of the best sleep he'd had in years. He hadn't intended to sleep in his car all night, and his neck was painfully stiff due to his awkward sleeping position, but boy did he feel refreshed.

He took the photo of the oak he'd propped up on the dashboard the night before, kissed it, and put it back in his wallet. He checked the time on his phone: 6:57 a.m. Kelly hadn't called him back. Why hadn't she called him? She understood the severity of the situation. Or maybe that was the problem—maybe she understood the severity of the situation so well that she'd gone to the police. Would she do that, though? Would she really sell her own husband down the river?

If it turned out that she had indeed given him up, Steve would just have to go on the lam. He had the rest of the cash he was going to pay the two men in his gym locker. He could go grab the cash, hit the road, and then drive to Mexico or Canada—whichever border was closer. And then he'd assume a new identity and open a seafood restaurant called *Cod Damnit*. Well, maybe he wouldn't open a restaurant—that might be too high-profile. But maybe he could find another secret lumberjack society that could offer him protection.

Steve's mind filled with dread as he thought about this new life that might await him. He didn't want to have to start over again, but if his wife had given him up, he would have no other choice.

Not entirely sure what his next move was going to be, Steve turned the ignition. He'd found that he usually got good ideas when he was driving. There was something about being in motion that really freed up his mind and allowed him to brainstorm effectively.

The problem was, Steve's car wouldn't start. Steve had a habit of driving with his headlights on during the day and he hadn't thought to turn them off last night since he hadn't planned on spending the evening in the parking lot.

And since he'd left his headlights on all night, his battery was now dead. He considered calling Kelly to ask her to bring the jumper cables, but he also knew he had to be wary of her. So instead he fished around in his wallet for his motor club card.

As Steve attempted to line up some roadside assistance, Kelly was entering their home, completely unaware that the two men were in their kitchen. She stopped in the doorway as she noticed the living room was in minor disarray. It was hard to tell whether Steve had thrown some things around in a fit or whether he just hadn't cleaned up after himself. Since the two men were such tidy ransackers, Kelly had no idea she was stepping foot into a ransacked house.

The two men stayed very quiet in the kitchen. As they heard Kelly walking toward them, the older brother clutched the knife that used to belong to Lenny.

"Steve?" said Kelly. "Steve, are you home?"

Kelly wasn't more than a few steps from entering the kitchen and receiving God-knows-what kind of reception from the two men when her phone rang. It was Steve. Kelly hadn't felt like talking to Steve yesterday, but she decided to take his call now. "Steve? Hold on, I'm going outside."

Kelly's phone didn't get good reception in their house, so she always had to go out to the driveway to talk on the phone. It was a nuisance, especially in the winter, but they were on a cheap plan and if they were to switch providers, their cell phone bill would double, so she put up with it. For whatever reason, Steve's phone always worked just fine in the house.

Maybe it wasn't the service, then—maybe Kelly just needed a newer phone. She used her phone so rarely, though, that she was never particularly motivated to upgrade her device.

Steve had decided to call Kelly after all. He'd found his motor club card only to discover it had expired over two years ago. Rather than renew his membership over the phone, he resolved to confront Kelly and find out exactly where he stood with her. And if he had to call her repeatedly until she picked up, so be it. But he could no longer stand being in a state of not knowing. Fortunately, Kelly picked up right away.

"Where are you?" said Kelly, now standing in the driveway.

"Where am I?" said Steve. "Where the hell are *you*?" Steve hadn't meant to start the conversation so combatively, but his neck was still sore and he hadn't eaten much in the last day or so and he was rather grouchy.

"I'm home," said Kelly. "I'm standing in the driveway. Where are you?"

Steve was not about to tell Kelly his whereabouts, at least not until he knew for sure that she hadn't reported him to the authorities.

"Did you go to the police?"

"What?"

"Did you go to the police? About that thing I told you about yesterday?"

"What? No, Steve. I didn't go to the police."

"Are you sure?"

"Yes, Steve. I'm sure. Now where are you?"

Steve had never known Kelly to lie to him, so he took her at her word. If Steve had known about Kelly's budding romance with Eric, he might not have been so quick to trust her, but as far as Steve knew, Kelly was still his loyal wife who would always be there for him.

190

"I'm in the parking lot at Pepe Muchacho's. Where the gas station used to be. My battery's dead. Do you still have those jumper cables in your trunk?"

"Yes."

"Would you mind giving me a jump?"

"I'm on my way."

Kelly got in her car and drove to the Mexican restaurant. She wondered why her husband had gotten himself into this murderous predicament. She normally would have grilled him about it when they'd spoken just now, but she felt like being nice to Steve today. She wasn't sure how you were supposed to act around your spouse after committing adultery for the first time, but she figured being polite was the best course of action for the time being.

In her haste to leave, Kelly had forgotten to shut the front door. The two men now stood in the doorway, perplexed by her abrupt departure. Had she figured out they were in the house? Was she on her way to the police station? They didn't want to stick around to find out, so the younger brother went back to the kitchen, grabbed the wooden boats, and then the two men left the house, shutting the door behind them.

48

Chester poked his head into the early morning yoga class. The class was taught by a woman named Ramona. When Chester had interviewed her for the position, he'd asked her if she was named after the character from the popular children's novels by Beverly Cleary. Up to that point in the interview, things had gone well, with Ramona sharing how she'd lived in India for two years to study yoga, and listing off the names of the yogis with whom she'd studied.

When Chester had asked her about the origin of her name and whether or not she'd been named after *that* Ramona, Ramona had simply smirked, as if she'd been answering that question her entire life. Then she just sat in silence with her arms crossed, making it clear she had no intention to reply. It wasn't until Chester moved on to the next question, which was something along the lines of why she thought she'd be a good fit for the gym, that she perked up again.

To this day, Chester didn't know whether or not she was named after the Ramona from the children's novels or not.

He caught her eye as she led the class through Bow Pose and waved to her with a smile. Ramona waved back, but made no attempt to smile. Chester didn't take it personally, though. He knew that while he was the kind of person who made an effort to smile several times a day, Ramona was not, and most likely never would be.

Chester continued down the hall to the men's locker room. Today was a special day for Chester because he'd decided he was going to swim for the first time in eleven years. The reason he'd decided he was going to swim for the first time in eleven years was because the day before he'd done something he normally never did—he'd smoked an entire pack of cigarettes.

On a normal day, Chester would usually smoke around five cigarettes. But yesterday he'd smoked five, and then he'd bought a new pack of cigarettes, and he smoked all those cigarettes, too.

He wasn't sure why he'd smoked all those cigarettes, other than he'd been feeling edgy all day. Maybe it was because of the two men who were asking about the pool and how the one man had lied about his age. Maybe it was because of his somewhat recent falling-out with Steve. Maybe it was because membership at the gym was down quite a bit. Maybe it was because he was lonely. Maybe it was because he hadn't traveled as much as he would have liked.

Whatever the reason, Chester had woken up feeling very unhealthy and immediately wanted to do something to counteract all the damage he'd done yesterday by smoking upwards of twenty-five cigarettes. So he grabbed an old pair of goggles and an equally old pair of swim trunks that he hadn't worn in a long, long time and drove straight to the gym.

After waving to Ramona and taking a quick shower, Chester made his way to the pool. He was surprised to find no one there, other than Tyler the lifeguard. Tyler was thirty years old and he would tell anyone who would listen that he was downright terrified of the water until he was fifteen and hadn't learned how to swim until he was seventeen.

As a child, he'd always been scared witless of drowning, but one day he decided to confront his demons and started taking lessons at the gym. As the years went by, Tyler eventually taught swimming lessons himself, and then when the former lifeguard left the position to take a job that actually paid decent money, Tyler took over the role. Tyler didn't care that he wasn't paid decent money. For him, simply being a lifeguard was the reward. He'd gone from being absolutely petrified of going into a swimming pool to becoming a lifeguard. To Tyler, that was the ultimate in personal transformation. One day he was going to write a book about it, but in the meantime he was too busy keeping swimmers alive.

Tyler was applying sunscreen as Chester approached him. Chester never understood why Tyler put sunscreen on since the pool was indoors. But Tyler had always been a character to say the least, so Chester never teased him about it.

"Well, look at this," said Tyler with a laugh. "Am I seeing what I think I'm seeing? Is that Chester in a swimsuit? Are you feeling okay?"

Chester smiled. "Morning, Tyler. Yep, you're seeing what you think you're seeing."

"And to what do we owe this pleasure?"

"Don't know, Tyler. Guess I just felt like going for a swim."

Tyler held his arms out. "Well, you got the place to yourself. Enjoy!"

Chester laughed and walked toward the deep end to swim some laps. As he was stretching, Tyler called out to him.

"Hey, Chester! Whatever happened to that Steve guy? That guy who was accusing people of peeing in the pool?"

"Still a member as far as I know."

"I haven't seen him around lately."

Chester shrugged. He didn't feel like talking about Steve. He felt like swimming laps. And since he hadn't been in a pool since forever, he felt like having some fun, too. So he put on his goggles, got a running start, and cannonballed into the pool, creating a giant splash.

Water flew everywhere. If it had been a regular gym member, Tyler would have blown his whistle and chastised him for causing a disturbance. But this was Chester; he was the manager, and a former competitive swimmer, so Tyler just laughed and playfully applauded the mess his boss made.

Chester surfaced, then went right into a breaststroke. After completing several laps, he transitioned to the butterfly. When he grew tired of that, he started doing a backstroke.

He knew he'd be sore as hell the next day, but for now it felt great to be back in the water. Why had he stayed away from it for so long? Pride was probably one of the reasons. In his prime, Chester had been one of the best swimmers in the country, if not the world. He had the medals and trophies to prove it, too. He didn't have any Olympic medals, but there wasn't any shame in that. Ninety-nine point nine percent of great swimmers didn't have Olympic medals. He did once qualify to swim at an Olympic trial, but that was as close as he got.

And he'd accomplished all of it with little to no support from his parents. He remembered on more than one occasion overhearing his mother quarrel with his father saying, "I wish we'd never signed him up for those damn swimming lessons." Neither of his parents understood why Chester felt compelled to swim so damn much. As far as they were concerned, swimming was something a boy did during the summer, not year-round.

His parents rarely attended his meets and never threw any kind of lavish celebrations for him when he won. It was up to Chester to find his way to and from the pool, as his parents regularly refused to drive him. Sometimes Chester's coaches would give him rides, otherwise he took the bus.

It wasn't until Chester landed a swimming scholarship at a fairly prestigious university that Chester's parents finally understood how certain benefits could be reaped from all this swimming nonsense. But Chester never took his studies particularly seriously. He wanted to be an Olympian! And he never did graduate, nor did he make an Olympic team.

As time went by and his racing speed diminished, it was hard for Chester to transition from the role of "competitive swimmer" to simply "swimmer." If he couldn't be one of the best at swimming, he didn't want to do it at all.

For his last few laps, he freestyled, pushing himself to see how fast he could go. It felt good to know that for once he wasn't being timed. It was just him out there and he could go as slow or as fast as he liked. But Chester always preferred going fast when it came to swimming, timer or no timer.

When he finally decided to call it quits, he pulled his goggles up to rest on his head, rubbed his eyes, and was surprised to be greeted by a round of applause.

As Chester was swimming off yesterday's consumption of cigarettes, as well as memories of never quite reaching his ultimate goal of becoming an Olympian, about a dozen gym members had gathered to watch.

Several of them had their phones out and were taking video and pictures. Most everyone who belonged to the gym knew Chester had been a competitive swimmer at one time, but no one had ever seen him in action.

"No pictures!" Chester joked. "And no autographs, either!"

Chester got out of the pool and wrapped a towel around himself. The applause continued and a few of the gym members offered Chester high-fives that he happily returned.

"Is this going to become a regular thing?" one of the members said. "Are we going to see you swimming all the time now?"

Chester smiled. "I don't know. I just felt like swimming today."

Then Chester went back to the locker room, got dressed, and set off to buy a fresh pack of cigarettes.

49

Approximately three years after Glen told Steve at that dinner that he wanted Steve to inherit the gas station, Glen died. Glen never did officially change his will to allow for Steve to inherit the gas station, so Glen's son inherited the gas station instead.

This was the same son who never checked in on Glen and never sent him a letter. And the son didn't attend Glen's funeral, either.

Steve and Kelly were devastated when Glen died, and they were devastated again when they learned that Steve was not going to inherit the gas station. Sure, the gas station's business had dropped off quite a bit since the two new service stations had opened, but it was still a fairly profitable business that had loyal customers like Sylvia, and Steve and Kelly had every intention of keeping the gas station open for the rest of their lives.

One evening, shortly after Glen's funeral, Glen's son came to the gas station and informed Steve that he was going to sell the gas station to developers and they were going to tear it down and build a Chinese restaurant in its place.

Steve did not like Glen's son. He wasn't particularly friendly. In fact, he wasn't friendly at all. And Steve didn't like that Glen's son didn't care about the gas station and that he hadn't attended Glen's funeral. Steve also didn't like the fact that a Chinese restaurant was going to take the gas station's place. Their suburb *already had* a Chinese restaurant. Who the hell thought it was a good idea to put in a second one?

"Hey, that's not up to me," said Glen's son when Steve asked him about the Chinese restaurant. "They can put in a strip club for all I care. The bottom line is your services are no longer needed here. So thanks for helping out my dad over the years, but you gotta go."

Glen's son wore a cashmere trench coat and expensive-looking gloves and his hair was perfectly parted to one side. He couldn't have looked any less like Glen if he'd tried.

"This gas station was your father's life," said Steve from behind the counter.

Glen's son sneered. "Was it? Was it, though? My dad hardly knew where he was half the time."

Even though he didn't like Glen's son one bit, Steve couldn't argue with him there. When Steve first met Glen it was true that he didn't know where he was half the time. And as the years went by, it became more like seventy-five percent or even ninety percent of the time that Glen didn't know where he was. But Steve wasn't about to let Glen's son know that. "Your dad knew where he was *more* than half the time. Of course, how would you know? You were never around."

Glen's son sneered again. He was very good at sneering. If there was such a thing as an International Sneering Competition, Glen's son would have participated in it annually and he would have finished first on multiple occasions.

"Just so we're clear," said Glen's son as he surveyed the candy bar selection in front of the counter, "this is your last night. Don't come back tomorrow." He then took a candy bar, put it in the pocket of his trench coat and left.

Steve looked out the window and saw a driver holding open the door to a black town car; Glen's son got in. As Steve watched him ride off, he saw Sylvia's Aspen pull into the station. She honked to let Steve know she wanted him to fill her tank.

As he walked to Sylvia's car, Steve was still steaming from his interaction with Glen's son. What a jerk that guy was. How could anyone not like Glen? Let alone his own kid?

Then Steve's mind turned to thoughts about his own father and how he and his dad rarely saw eye to eye on anything, yet Steve also knew there were plenty of people out there who liked his father because his father had helped them at one time or another.

Who knew what might have transpired between Glen and his son over the years? Maybe Glen was hard on him, or maybe he never took him fishing. Maybe Glen had been a womanizer, and maybe his son had disapproved of that type of behavior. Whatever it was, all Steve knew was he was out of a job and out of a retirement plan.

"I made you brownies," said Sylvia. She handed Steve a plate of chocolate brownies covered in plastic wrap.

"Wow, thank you, Sylvia." Steve wasn't really in the mood for brownies, but he graciously accepted them.

"You can go put them inside," said Sylvia. "I'll wait."

That sounded like a good idea to Steve since there wasn't really any place by the gas pumps to set down a plate of brownies. Sylvia liked the idea as well because that meant she'd get to look at Steve's butt twice that evening—once while he was putting away the brownies and again when Steve went to make her change.

Steve considered telling Sylvia that the gas station would be closing and would soon be replaced by a Chinese restaurant, but he didn't. He didn't give her any indication at all. He knew she'd just be disappointed and he didn't want to be the bearer of bad news. The only thing Steve did differently that evening was he didn't charge Sylvia for her gas.

"It's on the house," said Steve.

"On the *house*? That's no way to run a business. No, I insist." Sylvia waved a twenty-dollar bill at Steve.

"Sorry, Sylvia. Your money's no good here tonight."

Sylvia gave Steve a puzzled look, then shrugged and put the

money back in her purse. "Okay, well, thank you, I suppose. But I'm paying next time!"

"That's a deal," said Steve.

Sylvia was slightly disappointed she wouldn't have the opportunity to look at Steve's butt a second time now that he wouldn't be walking back to the store to make her change. At least she'd been able to see it earlier when he was putting away the brownies.

"And remember to share those brownies with your wife!" Sylvia said as she drove off.

Steve waved to Sylvia, then went inside the store and tried to figure out what to do next. This was his first time being a part of a business that would be closing forever the following day. Glen's son hadn't given Steve any specific instructions other than to leave and not come back, so maybe there wasn't anything left for Steve to do.

He took the cash out of the till and put it in the safe like he did every night. He briefly considered pocketing the money. Glen's son certainly wouldn't have noticed and Steve and Kelly could have used the extra cash to tide them over.

But Steve couldn't do that to Glen. He couldn't do that to a fellow lumberjack. So he just put the money away like he normally did. He was about to turn out the lights for the last time when a boy walked through the door.

His name was Alan and when Steve saw him, he knew exactly what he wanted—he wanted baseball cards. Alan never talked much; he would just put his change on the counter and Steve would count it out for him and tell him how many packs of baseball cards he could afford. Usually Alan would have enough change to purchase two packs.

Alan made his way to the counter, pulled his change out of his pocket, and Steve started counting it for him.

"A little late for you to be out, isn't it?"

Alan shrugged.

Steve didn't really care that Alan was out by himself in the evening. He was just teasing him a bit. He liked to try to get Alan to talk whenever he came to the gas station, but Alan was as shy as they came.

"Well, tonight's your lucky night," said Steve. "You've got enough for two packs, but we're running a special this evening: buy two, get the rest of the box free."

Steve pushed the box of cards toward Alan. The box wasn't full, but there were still probably thirty packs in there.

Alan put his hands around the box of baseball cards and stared at them. He then looked up at Steve in disbelief.

"Go ahead," said Steve. "They're all yours. Take some candy, too. You like licorice, right?"

Alan didn't take any candy. He didn't even take the baseball cards. He just stared at them a little longer and then slowly started shaking his head.

"It's okay," said Steve. "Take 'em."

Alan locked eyes with Steve as he continued to slowly shake his head. Then he pulled his change off the counter, put it back in his pocket and cautiously made his way to the exit, never once taking his gaze off Steve. Once comfortably outside, Alan got on his bike and pedaled off.

Alan's reaction stumped Steve. What kid wouldn't want a bunch of free baseball cards and candy? It certainly had been an unpleasant evening, starting with the unannounced visit from Glen's son and ending with Steve unintentionally terrifying Alan.

All Steve knew was he needed a drink. He considered bringing the brownies with him, but Steve had always equated brownies with celebrations and he certainly wasn't in a celebratory mood. So he left them behind the counter, next to the little black-and-white television Glen used to love. Maybe whoever was in charge of tearing down the gas station would want them.

Then he locked up and headed to the bar. Kelly would be upset to hear that it was Steve's last night as a gas station employee. Ever since the truth about Glen's will came out, they knew this day was coming, but the finality of it still stung.

Steve entered the bar, broke the news to Kelly, then sat down and ordered a drink from Ernie.

Steve drank that night until the bar closed and then he kept drinking frequently and abundantly for the next two decades. As he continued to drink, he became more and more miserable, eventually evolving into the jerk he was today.

At one point during those bleary decades, a young man wandered into the bar, sat down next to Steve and asked him if he knew where the town's secret lumberjack society was.

Steve looked up from his whiskey to see this young man had been worked over something fierce. He had two black eyes and upwards of seven missing teeth. Half of his head was shaved as well, for seemingly no good reason. This young man was a former lumberjack if ever there was one.

"I have no idea what you're talking about," said Steve, downing the last of his whiskey.

"Are you sure about that?" said the young man, proffering a fifty-dollar bill.

Steve took a good long look at the fifty-dollar bill. He could have used that money at that point in his life and all he had to do to earn it was help out a fellow lumberjack. And if he and this kid teamed up, maybe the two of them could grow the town's secret lumberjack society into something bigger than a gas station-turned-Chinese restaurant. Maybe they could become venture capitalists and invest in a chain of profitable laundromats. Maybe, just maybe, they could become the most financially successful former lumberjacks of all-time.

Steve mulled all this over before ultimately electing to shove the kid off his stool and telling him to get the hell out of his face or he would bite his nose off, shave the other half of his head, and shit down his throat.

50

"So how's *E*?" said Steve.

"What?" said Kelly.

"*E*," said Steve. "Eric. The guy you're screwing."

Kelly thought Steve could have been a bit more courteous, considering she'd just gone out of her way to help him jumpstart his car. She was under no obligation to have done that. She was also under no obligation to have accepted his phone call, but she'd done that, too. She was beginning to regret having helped him at all.

At the same time, she understood why Steve was angry. Their marriage was falling apart and she was indeed now carrying on a full-blown affair with another man.

And all of this was happening so close to their thirtieth wedding anniversary. It was a shame. But it also felt liberating. For the first time since she could remember, Kelly felt like she could move again. And now she had Eric in her life—a man who appreciated her carrot salads, and who, as far as she knew, was not arranging to have anyone killed.

Kelly knew she did not owe Steve any kind of explanation. He had unplugged from their marriage years ago. He'd spent decades drinking, and then when he finally sobered up, he replaced his alcohol obsession with Pizza Munch.

And now it appeared he was replacing his Pizza Munch obsession by fixating on Chester Rawlings, the manager of the gym Steve went to, who may or may not have been urinating in the gym's pool.

She was fed up. She was fed up watching her promising young husband, a man so skilled at breaking up fights, and so eager to transform a deteriorating gas station into a moderately successful gas station, wither away over the years.

She knew Steve's job placing bouncers at nightclubs never fulfilled him, but why hadn't he tried something different? She would have supported him emotionally, and she even would have gotten a job herself if that's what it would have taken to keep a roof over their heads while Steve transitioned to a line of work that made him happier.

But Steve had never wanted that. He wanted to be the one working. He wanted to be the one supporting them both. Maybe if Kelly had been more ambitious and had actually wanted to work, that would have changed things. It's not as if Steve *prevented* her from working. He just never encouraged her to work, and she never felt like getting another job after she quit her bouncer job since the tips had been so lousy.

Now, finally, she was feeling motivated to embark on a career for the first time in her life. She was priming herself to become a pharmacist. Sure, she knew she had a long way to go and that she might face intense questioning about her waitressing background, but she also knew the skills she was learning in her compliments class would be valuable and could perhaps even cancel out any doubts people might have regarding her involvement with that diner.

Of course, Kelly was also very aware of the great disdain Steve had for pharmacists, so while this was a career she was now excited about, she knew Steve would be downright disgusted if she told him about it and would not be happy for her at all.

Why did these things have to be so complicated? Why did she have to be inspired to become a pharmacist? Why couldn't she have been inspired to become a veterinarian or a secret shopper? Then she could have both a career *and* a marriage, instead of having to pick one or the other.

But was she really that interested in being married to Steve anyway? He constantly treated her like she was in his way, that she was a burden to him, and on top of that, she couldn't remember the last time he sincerely apologized for *anything.*

"I'm sorry," said Steve.

"What?" said Kelly.

"I'm sorry I said that. The *screwing* thing. I'm sorry."

Kelly couldn't believe what she was hearing. Her husband seemed to be apologizing to her.

"Thank you for coming here today. You didn't have to do that. I'm sorry I snapped at you. I'm just sick and tired of sleeping in strange places, and I'm sore. Last night I slept in the car, the night before that I slept at the kitchen table. I don't know what the hell's going on with me."

For the first time in forever, Kelly started to feel some real sympathy for Steve.

"I got fired, Kelly. I lost my job. I haven't been to work in a month."

Steve sure was full of surprises lately. "You haven't been to work in a month? Then what have you been doing during the day?"

Steve put his hands in his pockets, let out a sigh, and stared at the ground. "I don't know."

"What do you mean you don't know? Steve, how do you not know? What is going on with you?"

Steve didn't respond. Kelly wasn't sure who she was looking at. This man certainly resembled her husband, but she'd never known Steve to not have an answer for her, or at least not make some sort of snide remark. She'd never known him to just go quiet, but that's what he was doing.

Kelly looked at the Mexican restaurant and thought about how it used to be Glen's gas station. She remembered how she and Steve used to sleep in their car in the parking lot and tape the cardboard from the baseball card boxes over the windows when they wanted to have sex.

She looked across the way to where the bar used to be, where Steve drank all those years and where she'd made terrible money as a bouncer. The bar wasn't there anymore. It was a bank now. She watched someone get out of a red sedan and walk up to the ATM. She wondered where Ernie was these days and whether or not his perfect teeth were still perfect.

Steve finally spoke up. "I'm sick of it, Kelly. I'm just sick of it."

Steve was on the verge of tears. For a moment, Kelly thought about putting her hand on his shoulder, but she didn't. She wasn't sure if Steve would want that or if he'd recoil at her touch.

"I'm sick of losing all the time."

"Steve, you're not a loser."

"Nope, nope. Gotta disagree with you there," said Steve as he rubbed his nose. "I couldn't cut it as a lumberjack. I got screwed out of becoming an owner of a gas station. I was a drunk for a long time. Then I got fired again from a job a trained monkey could do. I got fired for accepting bribes, Kelly."

"Bribes?" said Kelly.

"Yes, Kelly. Bribes. I mean, pretty lousy bribes. We're talking bribes along the lines of the cut of the lousy tips you used to make at the bar, but bribes nonetheless."

Kelly shook her head. It was just too much. Everything that came out of her husband's mouth these days was just one bombshell after another. Sure, this accepting of bribes and termination from his job confession wasn't as shocking to her as the murder plot he'd divulged to her yesterday, but still, when would it end?

Now Kelly was tearing up. But she was also so flustered, she had to let out a laugh. "Anything else you want to share with me, Steve?" she said as she wiped a tear from her eye.

Steve let out a little laugh himself. "No, no. I think that's about it, other than I'm sorry I left you alone with my dad yesterday. With everything else going on, I just...."

Kelly laughed again. "It's okay. We actually had a fairly nice talk."

Kelly considered telling Steve about her desire to become a pharmacist, but then thought better of it. Steve was clearly in a tender place at the moment, and he might not want to hear that particular bit of news.

"I think I'm going to drive home," said Steve. "The tree's dying. You know, my mom."

This time Kelly did put her hand on Steve's shoulder. "Steve, I'm so sorry to hear that."

"Thank you."

Steve couldn't hold back his tears now. The sight of Steve crying made Kelly cry, too.

They stood there crying—Steve with his hands in his pockets, and Kelly with one hand on Steve's shoulder.

The manager of the Mexican restaurant pulled into the parking lot. He noticed the two middle-aged people in the corner of the parking lot standing and crying. He wasn't sure why they were crying, but he figured he'd give them approximately fifteen minutes to finish their business, at which point he'd confront them and let them know that the parking lot was for customers only, so if they weren't interested in at least purchasing a small fountain drink, they would have to leave.

51

Eric was experiencing a monster hangover. He hadn't drunk like that since college. He'd also slept until noon. He hadn't done that since college, either.

What time had he and Kelly gone to bed? He couldn't remember. He couldn't remember much after their dinner.

She wasn't there when he'd woken up, and as near as he could tell, she hadn't left a note, either. An overwhelming wave of sadness hit him when he first realized she'd left. Then panic set in. Had Eric said something unforgiveable to her when they were drinking?

He counted the four empty wine bottles in the kitchen. Boy, they'd sure gotten after it. But what a day they'd had! Lovemaking, a museum visit, a delicious dinner, and then drinking the night away like they were kids. He'd never experienced a day even remotely that fun with his wife.

His head was throbbing. He found a new bottle of wine, opened it, and poured himself a glass. He needed something to settle his nerves. He knew that drinking first thing in the morning might make someone think he was either an alcoholic or a serial killer, or both, but since there was currently no one present to observe his behavior, he allowed himself to do as he pleased.

He walked outside and sat down at the table where just last

night he and Kelly had cooked a delicious meal that would have pleased even the most critical panel of judges on one of those cooking competition shows.

As Eric sipped his wine, the realization set in that he was now a homewrecker. There was no way around it. He had initiated the homewrecking, too. What was he thinking showing up at Kelly's house like that? Why couldn't he have stayed away? Why hadn't he just gone on a dating website and rolled the dice with one of the many single women out there? Why did he have to choose Kelly?

He momentarily cursed Cliff, who'd been the one who'd encouraged him to take the compliments class in the first place, which had led to him meeting Kelly. But he then quickly realized there was no point in blaming a star for his misfortunes. Eric and Eric alone had made these recent choices. Cliff hadn't forced him to do any of it. All Cliff had done was offer his opinion.

If only he knew how Kelly was feeling and what she was thinking. Had she left because Eric had offended her? Did she leave because she felt guilty? Was she simply out picking up groceries so they could prepare a hearty breakfast? Should he go try to find her? Should he do nothing at all?

Eric thought about how he'd never had all that much luck in the love department. His wife wasn't particularly friendly, then she'd died unexpectedly, and now he was in love with a married woman.

He thought about his decision to enroll in a finders class, but wondered if that would also lead to adultery, just like the compliments class had. He couldn't stand the thought of falling for yet another married woman. No, Eric knew he had to show some restraint. No more falling in love for the time being. He would go to his finders class and he would learn all the cutting-edge techniques that would enable him to easily find any item he might misplace. He'd ace his exams, obtain his certificate of completion, and then sit back and enjoy all the additional time he would suddenly have since he would no longer be wasting that time trying to locate things.

Eric was beginning to feel much better about his life's direction. He even considered pouring himself another glass of wine. It was a lovely day and he was going to enjoy it, even if he didn't know where Kelly was or whether or not she was mad at him. He was going to be fine. He was going to stay in the moment and enjoy the moment. Que sera, sera.

Eric was able to stay in the moment for approximately ninety seconds, then his thoughts turned back to Kelly and the wave of sadness he'd recently experienced returned with a force three times stronger than before, and he knew for a fact it wouldn't matter how much wine he drank or how many new classes he enrolled in, he would not be able to get Kelly out of his mind anytime soon.

He started sweating; breathing became difficult. He worried he might be having a heart attack. Then he realized it wasn't a heart attack, but he would need to throw up as soon as possible. He raced back into his house, pulled up the lid on the toilet, fell to his knees, forcibly emptied the contents of his stomach, and passed out on the bathroom floor.

There was no getting around it: Eric had wolf love for Kelly, and any pleasure one derived from wolf love was always balanced out by generous helpings of agony, suffering, and pain.

52

The two men were standing outside the gym. They were in a good mood. They had to admit, they'd had a good amount of fun the past few days. They were smiling more, and they were smoking again.

While they'd enjoyed meeting Chester and were thankful to him for the discount he'd given them on their gym memberships, as well as the cigarettes he'd kindly provided them, they realized the time had come to kill him.

Chester knew too much. He knew they'd lied about their ages, and for all they knew, he'd already reported them to the police. They really did like Chester, but any thoughts they might have had before about letting him live and simply taking the money from Steve no longer seemed prudent. It was clear the right move now was to eliminate him.

So they would carry out the plan as Steve had originally laid it out for them—they would kill Chester and then Steve would pay them the remainder of the fifty-four thousand. Then they would be on their way, most likely retire from the killing business, and eventually open a public horse ranch that also offered hot air balloon rides.

But before they killed Chester and started the next chapter of their lives, they first wanted to have a cigarette outside the gym.

They owned a red lighter now, and if any pretty woman walked by looking for a light, the men would be more than happy to oblige her.

And only about a minute after they lit up, they were pleased to see Daphne, the bubbly young woman they'd met the other day, approach them.

"Hey, guys!" said Daphne, eying their cigarettes. "Mind if I bum one of those?"

"Certainly," said the older brother. He offered Daphne his pack and then lit her cigarette with his red lighter.

Kelly took a drag and let out a very satisfied-sounding exhale. "Thanks so much. I was craving a cigarette so bad. I think I'm entitled to one before I go in there and get my ass kicked."

The two men knew Daphne was referring to her Pilates class. She'd mentioned the other day that it always gave her a real good ass-kicking.

"Happy to be of service," said the older brother. "So, how long have you been a member here?"

"Oh, about three years?"

"That's great," said the older brother. "My brother and I just joined."

"Whoa!" said Daphne. "That's so cool! Welcome! You're gonna love it here. Everyone is so friendly."

Just then, the older brother's phone rang. Steve was calling. *Jesus Christ*, he thought. *What does he want now?*

The older brother did not want to talk to Steve at all. He just wanted to finish his cigarette, maybe get Daphne's phone number, and kill Chester. He handed his phone to his younger brother. "It's you-know-who. Here, talk to him."

The younger brother didn't want to talk to Steve, either. He wanted to talk to Daphne and he was more than a little ticked at his older brother for hogging the conversation. He had plenty of thoughtful and insightful things to share with her if only his brother would let him get a word in edgewise.

But his older brother had already gone back to talking to

Daphne and she seemed to be buying his B.S., so the younger brother realized he might as well talk to Steve since he'd quickly become a third wheel.

"What?" said the younger brother as he walked away from his older brother and Daphne.

"I'm calling it off," said Steve.

"Calling what off?"

"You know, the thing! What else would I be calling off?"

"You're saying you don't want us to do it?"

"Yes! That's exactly what I'm saying. Don't do it."

"Well, what about the rest of the money?"

"Yeah, I thought about that," said Steve, "and I'm willing to offer you a buyout. How does twenty thousand sound?"

"Twenty grand?" said the younger brother. "That doesn't sound like enough. Besides, we don't do buyouts. We only do original offers."

Truth be told, the two brothers had accepted a buyout once. It was about twelve years ago in Arizona, but it had proved to be a real pain in the neck, and after it was over, they vowed to never accept a buyout again.

"Come on," said Steve, "I don't want to do it anymore. I've had a change of heart. How about twenty-four thousand?"

"How about *no*?" said the younger brother. The younger brother was getting pretty fed up with Steve. He had always wanted to retire more than his older brother. He was sick and tired of dealing with these flakes. First they wanted someone killed, then they didn't want someone killed. Why the hell couldn't they make up their goddamn minds? Who were these people? Didn't they realize it was their indecisiveness that got them into these situations in the first place? If they'd just commit to something and see it through, they'd be fine. But they couldn't leave well enough alone. They always had to meddle, and the younger brother was sure as hell done holding their hands.

As Steve continued to insist on a buyout, the younger brother turned his attention back to his older brother who seemed to really be hitting it off with Daphne. His older brother had always had a way with the ladies and he appeared to be working his magic once again.

"No," said the younger brother in response to Steve's latest offer, which was now up to twenty-six thousand eight hundred. "Too many people have knowledge."

"What does that mean?" said Steve.

"It means what it means," said the younger brother.

Under less stressful circumstances, Steve and the younger brother might have gotten onto the topic of their ages and made the connection that they were both fifty-two. If the conversation had gone that way, they might have bonded over being the same age and maybe the younger brother would have felt like he could have trusted Steve a bit more and then maybe he and his brother would have been able to accept a buyout after all.

But the conversation didn't go that way. In fact, the topic of their age never came up once. The conversation just kept making the younger brother angrier and angrier, and watching his older brother hitting it off with Daphne also made him angrier and angrier, and truth be told, the younger brother wasn't so happy to be smoking again. He knew full well the damaging effects smoking could have on a person's body. That's why he'd quit in the first place. Maybe his brother was enjoying puffing away on those cancer sticks again, but he was realizing he didn't want to smoke anymore and he didn't want to open a public horse ranch that also offered hot air balloon rides.

And why had they been smiling so much lately? The younger brother *hated* smiling. He'd only been smiling lately because his brother had been smiling. But he was getting sick of that, too.

He just wanted to finish this job and then go his own way. He was fed up with living in his older brother's shadow. He was fifty-two for God's sake and if he wasn't going to become his own man now, when would he ever?

All these thoughts bombarded the younger brother and gave him a tremendous headache. He threw his cigarette to the ground and stomped it out. He was done smoking. After they took care of Chester, he was done killing, too. And he was definitely done following his older brother around everywhere.

"Alright, listen," said the younger brother. "Meet us at the Pizza Munch parking lot in an hour." He then hung up the phone.

Steve didn't know whether that meant the brothers were accepting his buyout offer of $26,800 or not, but it sounded like they were going to take it, and that meant Chester would live, too, which was a relief to Steve. Now that he was seeing things more clearly, he realized killing Chester wouldn't solve anything.

While Steve was feeling clear-headed, the younger brother was feeling enraged and vengeful. All the suppressed animosity he'd been harboring toward his brother over the years was now bubbling to the surface. He hadn't realized how much he truly disliked his older brother until now and he could not wait to get away from him.

But first, he knew what had to be done: they had to kill Chester and they also had to kill Steve. Too many people had knowledge and they had to be terminated.

Then he'd go his own way. He wouldn't tell his brother, either. He'd just leave.

Daphne and the older brother were finishing up their conversation as the younger brother approached them.

"Well, time for my ass kicking!" said Daphne. "Thanks for the smoke!"

Daphne waved to the two brothers as she walked inside the gym.

"Not bad," said the older brother as he watched Daphne walk away. "Not bad at all." He then turned to his younger brother. "What'd he say?"

"He's gotta go," said the younger brother.

"I'd been thinking that, too."

"I told him to meet us at the Pizza Munch parking lot in an hour."

"Works for me."

The older brother put out his cigarette and the two men entered the gym.

53

Fortunately for Chester, he was not at the gym. He was at a birthday party.

The birthday party was being thrown for a boy named Harold. It was Harold's seventh birthday and all the guests were being entertained by a reptile handler who was showing everyone the proper way to pet an iguana. The iguana's name was Sparky and he was a real hit with everyone present.

Harold's parents were long-time gym members and when they saw Chester swimming in the pool earlier in the day, they invited him to Harold's birthday party.

Chester wasn't all that interested in reptiles, so he stood by himself in a corner of the yard, smoking a cigarette. Nobody cared that Chester smoked at the gym since everyone there liked him so much, and that went for smoking at children's birthday parties as well.

Chester finished his cigarette around the time the reptile show was wrapping up. He pulled out a travel-size bottle of hand sanitizer and rubbed it on his hands. Harold's mother noticed and asked Chester if she could have some sanitizer as well.

"Of course," said Chester. He handed her the bottle.

"Do you mind if I let the kids use it, too?" said Harold's mom. "We're about to have cake and the kids just touched all those reptiles."

"There's plenty for everyone," said Chester.

The kids formed a line and took turns rubbing sanitizer on their hands. Then Harold's mom told all the kids to give Chester a hug and to thank him for allowing them to use his hand sanitizer.

Chester was having a great day. He was still coming down from the high of swimming for the first time in eleven years, and now he was on the receiving end of a group hug. He'd been so stressed the other day, but now he was feeling much better about things.

He thought to himself that he would definitely start swimming again on a regular basis. It was okay for him to just be a regular swimmer and not be a competitive swimmer; there was no shame in that. Maybe he'd even start taking up gym members on their offers to race. Why not?

Harold's father brought out the cake and everyone started singing. Chester joined in. He was happy he'd decided to attend Harold's party. Going to a child's birthday party wasn't something he normally did, but up until this morning, swimming wasn't something he normally did, either.

And it was a good thing Chester switched up his routine on this particular day, otherwise the gym would have been dealing with a dead gym manager and there wouldn't have been anyone at Harold's party to offer hand sanitizer to the kids.

Harold's mother felt bad about pestering Chester for his hand sanitizer. She'd first asked the reptile handler for some, but the handler didn't have any. And what really ticked off Harold's mother was that the handler didn't offer any kind of excuse for not providing sanitizer. Instead, she actually gave Harold's mother a look that implied that Harold's mother was in the wrong for having asked her for sanitizer in the first place!

Thankfully, Chester's sanitizer saved the day, but Harold's mother was already plotting her revenge. She didn't care how tired and worn out she'd be at the conclusion of Harold's party; she would still summon the strength to sit down at her computer and write a very thorough online review, letting the entire world know how "average" her experience with this reptile company had been.

When it came to keeping children's hands clean, Harold's mother didn't fuck around.

54

Kelly was at home, packing. She'd just gotten off the phone with Jennifer, her compliments class instructor. They'd had a nice talk. Kelly apologized for calling her on a weekend and when Jennifer told her she didn't mind, Kelly complimented her on her patience and willingness to help her students regardless of what day of the week it was.

Kelly had called Jennifer to ask for an extension on taking the final. She explained to her that due to a "family emergency" she had to leave town immediately and was almost positive she wouldn't be back in time to take the final on Thursday.

Jennifer complimented Kelly on taking the initiative to call her and let her know what was happening. She told Kelly to take as much time as she needed and that the exam would be waiting for her when she returned. And if it took as long as seven years for the family emergency to sort itself out, the exam would still be waiting for her.

"The most important thing is that you just make sure you keep complimenting at least ten people every day," Jennifer told Kelly.

Kelly assured Jennifer she would keep hitting her daily quota.

As Kelly packed, she continued to notice that things in their house seemed to be a little bit disorganized (she still wasn't aware that the two men had conducted their gentle ransacking), but she shrugged it off and continued filling her suitcase.

She wasn't sure where she was going to go next, but once she and Steve had finished crying in the parking lot, they both agreed that Steve had put them in a very bad situation by calling the two men into their lives and therefore they'd both better disappear for a while—perhaps even for as long as seven years. They'd sell the house eventually, but for now what was most important was their safety.

They drove to the gym so Steve could get the remainder of the cash out of his locker. Steve confessed to Kelly that he'd already paid the two men seventy-two hundred dollars, which had left him with approximately forty-six thousand eight hundred in cash. He'd offered to split the remaining amount with Kelly, but she told him to just give her twenty thousand and he could keep the rest. Kelly didn't like doing math and preferred to work with round numbers—that was the main reason she'd only requested twenty thousand.

And that was the main reason why Steve had offered the two men a maximum buyout of twenty-six thousand eight hundred—because that was all the money he had left.

Even though Kelly had recovered from the initial shock of Steve telling her about his murder plot and was now dealing with it in a more measured way, she was still furious with Steve. She knew he'd had his head up his ass for the past several years, but she had no idea it had been *that* far up his ass.

What a dummy, thought Kelly. *What a putz! What a loser!*

Fortunately, Kelly caught herself having negative thoughts and put the kibosh on that immediately. She'd promised Jennifer she would make her compliments quota every day, and even though Kelly was under a considerable amount of stress, she would not forget that all-important acronym from her compliments training:

A.B.C. = Always Be Complimenting

She shifted gears and forced herself to see Steve in a positive light. At least he'd come to his senses and decided to call the thing off. She had to give him credit for that. And during their recent interaction in the parking lot, he'd talked to her in a respectful manner for the first time in ages. Finally, he was once again communicating with her as if she was someone he loved and not some kind of annoying object that was constantly in his way.

Kelly let out a chuckle. She had to. She was having trouble accepting that this was her life. If someone had told her when she was forty-four years old that she'd be fleeing from two contract killers hired by her husband, she would have told that person they were nuts!

But here she was, preparing to flee. At least she had Eric, and she had to admit they did have wolf love. But wolf love also had a tendency to quickly burn itself out. Could she and Eric sustain a long-term relationship based on wolf love alone? And what if Eric was angry with her for having left after a full day of romance without even leaving a note?

She'd have to talk to him before she left town. But first she needed something to eat. She went to the kitchen and whipped herself up a carrot salad.

She sat down at the kitchen table and noticed the wooden boats Steve's father had given them were no longer there. Maybe Steve had moved them. Or maybe he'd thrown them out. She knew only too well how much Steve loathed his father and his wooden boats.

But she didn't have time to think about wooden boats at a time like this. She was in full-on survival mode. The carrot salad was helping her feel a little bit better, but she was still under a tremendous amount of stress.

She knew, however, that if she was ever going to become a pharmacist, she had to learn to live with being stressed out all the time. Steve's father had warned her that was part of the job. But he'd also told her that as long as she possessed ingenuity, courage, and a tremendous amount of self-respect, she'd be okay.

Plus, when she retired from her pharmacist career, she was

guaranteed to have at least two million dollars in her bank account.

And even if two million dollars didn't go as far as it used to, who in their right mind wouldn't want to be a millionaire?

55

The two men searched the gym high and low, but had no luck finding Chester. They eventually decided to let themselves into his office and wait for him to return.

As the two men sat there, the older brother sensed that something was wrong with his younger brother. He was being oddly quiet. Sure, the two men never spoke to each other all that much anyway, but something about his younger brother's silence seemed more silent than usual.

"Everything okay?" said the older brother.

"Yeah," said the younger brother.

The older brother was glad that he'd taken the time to clear the air. They normally didn't have those kinds of heart-to-heart talks where they discussed each other's feelings, but his brother's feelings were important to him, even if he never really told him that they were.

Tyler, the gym's lifeguard, walked into Chester's office to drop off his timecard.

"Oh, hey," said Tyler. "I'm just dropping something off for Chester." He set his timecard down on Chester's desk.

"Are you growing a goatee?" Tyler said to the younger brother.

The younger brother shot Tyler a look. Who the hell was this guy and why was he asking him about his goatee? Yes, he was growing a goatee, but he didn't feel like talking about it. He was going through a big transition in his life. He had a couple more people to kill and then he was going to abandon his older brother for good. Still, in the interest of not calling any undo attention to himself or his brother, he felt the best course of action was to be pleasant.

"Yes," said the younger brother. "I'm growing a goatee."

"I knew it!" said Tyler. He then pointed at the older brother. "Well, when it comes in, I hope it's half as good as your friend's goatee because that is a really solid goatee."

The older brother was also not in the mood to discuss goatees, but he also knew that when you were on the verge of killing someone that it wasn't wise to call undo attention to yourself by behaving in an angry or peculiar way, so he acknowledged Tyler's compliment.

"Thank you," said the older brother. "I also hope it's half as good as mine."

Tyler applied some lip balm and smiled at the two men. "Well, have a good one!" He turned to leave.

"Hey," said the older brother, "you wouldn't happen to know where Chester is, would you?"

"Oh, are you guys waiting for Chester? Yeah, I think he's at Harold's birthday party. Do you guys know Harold?"

The two men shook their heads. They did not know Harold.

"Yeah, Chester was swimming today and I overheard Harold's parents invite him to Harold's party. Do you want me to get you their address?"

"That would be great," said the younger brother.

"No problemo," said Tyler. Tyler sat down at Chester's desk and accessed the gym's membership database. This was certainly not something he should have been doing. If Chester and Harold's parents knew he was doing this, they would have been irate and Harold's parents probably would have encouraged Chester to fire Tyler. But Tyler didn't know he shouldn't have been giving out this information; he just thought he was being helpful. Plus, he wanted to impress the men with his computer skills.

"Here, I'll write it down for you." Tyler wrote down the address on a nearby scrap of paper and handed it to the older brother.

"Thank you," said the older brother. "You've been very helpful."

"Hey, I aim to please!" said Tyler with a laugh.

The two men stood up and left. Tyler felt good about what he'd done. Chester was always telling the gym employees to be friendly to the members, and whenever possible, to go out of their way to make the members' gym experience as pleasant as possible. Tyler had recognized this as an opportunity to help out some members and he'd taken full advantage of it.

56

Steve was sitting in his car in the Pizza Munch parking lot. He'd been spending a lot of time in parking lots lately and he was getting sick of it. Thankfully, he wasn't *living* in a parking lot like he'd once done when he and Kelly were younger, but he decided that after he completed the buyout he would avoid any and all parking lots for the foreseeable future.

But at least he was eating Pizza Munch pizza! He couldn't resist going inside and ordering a deep dish supreme to go. He'd been through a lot recently and needed to keep his blood sugar up. He knew eating all this pizza without balancing it out by going to the gym was not good for him in the short-term, but the time would eventually come when he could get back to eating better and working out more frequently.

He considered writing his father a letter to let him know he'd be making the drive home to chop down the oak tree, but then he thought about how his father hadn't given him any kind of heads-up before invading his and Kelly's lives, so why should he extend the old man the courtesy?

Steve had to admit that once his initial rage at seeing his father had passed, the interaction they had really hadn't been all that bad. Sure, he hadn't been overly friendly to his father and had told him he didn't want to see him in person anymore, but he'd said far worse things to his father over the years and they were still able to maintain a frigid, long-distance relationship where they went years without communicating with each other.

At the end of the day, his dad was his dad, and even though his father had that strange diner phobia and didn't like baseball gloves and had a weird obsession with painting wooden boats, there was a part of Steve that was becoming open to the idea of reconnecting with him, and if given the opportunity, he would strongly consider meeting with him in person more frequently.

His father wasn't the person he'd remembered him being. When Steve was eighteen, his father was an intimidating presence. Seeing him yesterday, though, he wasn't intimidated by him at all. He was annoyed to see him, sure, but not intimidated. Yesterday all he'd seen was a lonely, stubborn old man who apparently missed his son and was sad that the oak tree in his yard was dying.

As Steve sat there eating his pizza and thinking about his father, he didn't know whether he was truly interested in reconnecting with him or whether he was simply forcing himself to see his father in a positive light in the event he might need to live with him for an extended period of time.

Time would tell, but for now Steve was keeping all his options open. He knew he didn't want to go back to his own house; he didn't even want to go back there to pick up his cologne. He just knew he wanted to pay off the two men and then get to his father's house as soon as possible. He could pick up a new bottle of cologne along the way.

"Shit," Steve said out loud as he thought about the cologne. He hadn't budgeted in cologne money, or gas money for that matter. He'd told the men he was going to give them twenty-six thousand eight hundred dollars, which would leave him with absolutely nothing. And come to think of it, he'd just spent some of that money on the pizza he was eating, so there was no way now he could possibly give them the full amount.

So Steve decided his only option was to play hardball. When the men arrived, he would tell them he misspoke earlier and that the new offer was twenty-six thousand and they could take it or leave it. And if they had a problem with that, Steve would tell them he was deducting the eight hundred they'd made him leave for them outside the Pizza Munch the other day for no good reason. *Yeah, two can play at that game*, thought Steve. They weren't the only ones who could spring an eight-hundred-dollar demand on someone. Steve was capable of doing that, too!

His thoughts then turned to Kelly. Would she be a part of his future? He wasn't sure. He felt he'd like her to be, but they'd grown so far apart over the years. Was their marriage really worth fixing? *Could* it be fixed? Could Steve *change*? Did he *want* to change? Could Kelly ever forgive Steve for arranging to have Chester murdered?

In spite of all the uncertainty, Steve was hopeful. He was hopeful that good things would soon be coming his way. Steve hadn't felt hopeful since he got screwed out of inheriting the gas station, and he had to admit, feeling hopeful felt a hell of a lot better than feeling angry and vengeful. Perhaps that would be his new approach to life: hopefulness. He knew he'd have to work at it, but maybe, just maybe, he could change after all.

But before he dedicated himself to becoming more hopeful, Steve had to finish up this business with the two men. Sure, he could have hit the road without giving them another cent, but Steve was not going to put himself in a situation where the two men might think of him as a quitter. No, he would see this through to the end, even if it left him with only eight hundred dollars to his name. But under no circumstances would anyone ever be able to accuse him of being a quitter.

Steve was already working on becoming more hopeful, and he was hopeful that things with the two men would go well. However, just in case things didn't go well, Steve was glad he had a gun in the trunk of his car. The gun had belonged to Glen. Glen kept it behind the counter at the gas station. He never once had to use it, but he kept it there just in case.

Steve took the gun home with him the night Glen's son told Steve his services were no longer needed. Steve knew it was childish of him to have taken it, but he really didn't like Glen's son at all and felt the need to take something, so he took the gun. He never told Kelly about the gun. He figured she wouldn't want a gun in the house, so he kept it hidden in the basement for years.

The gun was old and Steve had never once fired a gun in his life and he didn't know if the gun even worked and he didn't know how things would go in the event he'd have to use it on the two men, but he also felt confident that he could figure it out pretty quickly if he had to. How difficult could it be to fire a gun?

Thinking about firing the gun made Steve feel queasy. He set down his pizza and looked at the time. The men would be arriving in approximately twenty minutes.

Steve got out of the car and took the gun out of the trunk. Then he sat back down in the driver's seat and wondered if he shouldn't order one more supreme pizza for the road. He had a long drive ahead of him.

57

The two men were walking to Harold's house. His house wasn't all that far from the gym. The younger brother looked at his watch and realized that even if they got to Harold's party and killed Chester immediately, they would still probably be late to their buyout appointment with Steve.

The younger brother didn't care, though. He didn't care if Steve had to wait. He just wanted to get everything over with so he could abandon his brother and start the next chapter of his life.

The older brother was thinking about the nice conversation he'd had with Daphne and he was also feeling a bit sad that due to recent developments he and his brother could no longer realistically expect to become gym members. He really had enjoyed himself quite a bit the past few days; hopefully he and his brother could join another gym in another town. The thought of joining another gym made him smile. He really was smiling a lot more these days and he felt good doing it.

The two men didn't realize they were being followed by Charlie. Charlie was the homeless person who Lenny had stabbed in the leg that one time when Charlie had asked Lenny where he got his incense.

Charlie had witnessed the two men kill Lenny, and that hadn't sat well with him. Lenny might have stabbed Charlie that one time, but Lenny was also the closest thing Charlie had to a friend, and he certainly didn't appreciate the two men killing the one person in the world who he could sort of refer to as a friend.

At the time, Charlie felt powerless to do anything. The men were big and seemed to be very adept at killing people. If he'd taken action at that moment, they most certainly would have overpowered him. So Charlie momentarily laid low, but soon came up with a plan. He knew he would need a gun. Charlie didn't own a gun, but he knew how to get one.

He would borrow Hank's gun. He knew Hank—the liquor store owner who offered some of the worst specials anyone had ever seen—kept a gun behind the counter. He also knew if he were to ask Hank if he could borrow it, there was no way in hell Hank would have obliged. So Charlie decided he would borrow it without Hank's knowledge and then return it after he'd done what he needed to do.

Charlie was very skilled at shoplifting. He shoplifted from Hank's store on a regular basis. Hank never once caught on since Charlie was so good at it. What he'd do was he would beg for change during the day, and then when he had enough money to buy a few things, he'd visit Hank's store.

At that point, he would purchase a few items and also steal a few items. The secret to Charlie's success was that he never got too greedy. So if he stole three things, he also bought three things. And he never stole anything he couldn't easily stash in one of his pockets.

Hank never caught on. In fact, Hank sort of liked Charlie. And that was saying a lot, since Hank didn't really like anyone. Hank didn't even really like himself.

Earlier in the day, Charlie entered the store like he normally did and walked around for a while like he normally did before he bought anything. Hank didn't think much of Charlie's loitering since he sort of liked Charlie to begin with and also because he knew once a homeless person entered your store, they tended to take their time before they left. He knew that for most homeless people, being in a liquor store was the highlight of their day.

Fortunately for Charlie, his timing couldn't have been much

better. He'd barely been in the store for a minute when a couple of teenagers walked in and immediately started making fun of Hank's specials.

"Wow!" exclaimed one of the teenagers in a very sarcastic tone. "If I buy one candy bar, I can get a second candy bar for two cents off!"

"Or how about this?" said the other teenager. "Apparently if you buy three packs of unsalted almonds, you can get a fourth pack for five percent off!"

"Man, it's our lucky day!" said the first teenager.

Hank, who already knew very well that his specials were not very good but was also incredibly thin-skinned when anyone teased him about them, immediately escalated the situation. "Listen, you shits, the specials are what they are. And if you don't like 'em, you can get the hell out of here."

Hank was still fuming from the memory of the two men making fun of his specials the other day. He knew that with those two men there was nothing he could say to them because he had a strong feeling that if he'd talked back to them, things wouldn't have gone well for him. But with these boys, he could say whatever he wanted. Hell, if he wanted to, he knew he could kick both their asses without even breaking a sweat.

The teenagers started laughing at Hank and that sent Hank into an apoplectic rage. If these boys wanted a fight, then they were going to get one. Hank ran around the counter and chased the boys out of his store and down the block.

Charlie saw his opportunity and ran behind the counter and grabbed Hank's gun. He then waited for Hank to return to the store and purchased a pack of gum so Hank wouldn't suspect him of anything.

"Those kids sure were assholes, huh?" said Charlie.

"I don't want to talk about it," said Hank. Hank seemed embarrassed for having lost his cool. He wiped the sweat off his forehead, gave Charlie his change, and then retreated to the office in the back of the store. There was no way to sugar coat it—Hank was an unhappy person and this go-round with the teenagers hadn't made him any happier.

There was a homeless shelter near the gym that Charlie frequented for coffee and soup. After finishing his soup and taking his coffee to go, Charlie spotted the two men in the gym's courtyard. One of them was talking to a bubbly young woman and the other was talking on the phone.

Charlie then watched them enter the gym. He had the gun now, but didn't think it would be a good idea to shoot the men inside the gym. There would be too many people around. So instead he waited for them to leave the gym, and then he trailed behind them for several blocks.

Charlie had never killed anyone before, but it turned out he was fairly good at it.

The two men were passing by Hank's liquor store when Charlie fired the gun and shot both men in the back. The men fell to the ground and didn't move at all. They didn't even twitch. They just died. Blood pooled on the sidewalk by their bodies. There was a lot of blood—definitely more blood than Charlie had ever seen at one time before.

Charlie started shaking. He hadn't thought about what he would do after he killed the men. Then it occurred to him that he should take their possessions. Since he was homeless, he could of course use whatever items they had on them. He turned the first man over and found a wad of cash in his pocket. Charlie couldn't tell how much money there was. He'd count it later, but it appeared to be in the thousands!

He then found two wooden boats in the pockets of the other man's coat. He wasn't sure why this man would be carrying these boats around. Maybe they were valuable? Maybe they were antiques? At any rate, Charlie took those, too.

He also found guns on them, so he took those as well. And he took their phones and their watches and their wallets. There was so much to carry!

Charlie dumped out a nearby garbage can, pulled out the liner, and filled it with his stash. He then hurried away.

Since the shootings took place right by Hank's store, Hank heard the gunshots. But Hank was too miserable to walk outside to see what had happened. He had enough problems defending his store's terrible specials to unappreciative customers. The last thing he needed was another hassle. Hank was too miserable to even notice that his gun was missing. Instead, Hank once again walked to the office in the back of the store and shut the door.

58

Kelly was sitting on Eric's couch. Eric's head was in her lap and she was stroking his forehead. Eric was experiencing a terrible hangover, just as Kelly knew he would. Kelly had considered leaving town, but then decided against it. Instead she went back to Eric's house and told him everything. Eric was having trouble thinking clearly since he was so hungover, but he thought that perhaps Kelly should go into the witness protection program.

"I thought about that, too," said Kelly. "But I don't know if I can be in the witness protection program and also be a pharmacist, and if given the choice between the two, I'd much rather be a pharmacist."

"I bet you could do both," said Eric.

"Maybe, but I don't want to risk it. I could really use that two million."

"Well, you can stay here as long as you like. Me and Cliff will protect you."

Kelly laughed. "You're cute."

"Thank you for the compliment. You're beautiful."

Kelly leaned forward and kissed Eric.

"I can't believe you're not hungover," said Eric.

"I don't get hangovers. No one in my family does."

Eric sat up. "Speaking of families, I'm sorry if I'm wrecking yours. I don't want to be a homewrecker."

Kelly sighed. "You're not a homewrecker. If anyone's a homewrecker, it's me. I probably got it from my mother. She was a homewrecker. She never intended to become one. It just sort of happened. It wasn't her fault, but she never got over it."

"I'm sorry," said Eric.

"Don't be," said Kelly. "Don't be sorry. Don't be anything. Let's just enjoy our wolf love."

They kissed, and then Eric rested his head back on Kelly's lap. Kelly ran her fingers through his hair. She was happy to be with Eric, but she was also thinking about Steve.

She hoped he'd be okay. Before leaving the house, she'd gone down to the basement to see if the gun Steve had never told her about was still there. It wasn't, and Kelly wasn't sure if that was a good sign or a bad one.

59

The men were forty-five minutes late, and Steve's patience was wearing thin. His nerves were fairly frayed as well. He'd never been in a shootout before and the thought that he might be forced to engage in one had his adrenaline soaring. At least the men's tardiness had given Steve time to go back into Pizza Munch and order a second pizza for the road.

Was this part of their plan? Were the men playing mind games? Were they secretly observing him from the far end of the parking lot?

Steve decided to call them. He wasn't going to get pushed around by these dirt bags any longer. In fact, he wasn't even sure if they were still worthy of a buyout. He dialed the number, but it immediately went to voicemail. He called again and got the same response. Then he called again and again and again.

Steve didn't know that Charlie had shot the men and taken their belongings. Shortly after killing them, Charlie decided to throw the men's phones in a nearby lake. Their phones looked cheap anyway, and Charlie didn't think he could get much for them if he decided to pawn them, so he opted to just get rid of them. He tossed the wooden boats in the nearby lake as well, once he determined they probably weren't antiques and were therefore most likely "unpawnable."

He'd also thrown the men's guns in the lake, as well as Hank's gun. Charlie felt bad about throwing Hank's gun away, but he realized the gun was a murder weapon now and it was in his best interest to get rid of it. And while he was pitching Hank's gun in the lake, he decided he might as well throw away the men's guns, too.

He'd gone through the men's wallets—both men had several IDs each! Who were these guys? Charlie decided he'd burn the wallets and IDs later. The only things he kept were the men's watches and the cash. He would pawn the watches; he knew a guy who he knew he could trust to not screw him over.

He also decided he would eventually mail Hank some cash to cover the cost of the gun. Even though he'd stolen plenty of items from Hank over the years, he felt like he'd crossed a line by stealing his gun. So the least he could do would be to reimburse him for that. He figured four hundred dollars would be sufficient.

Steve had no idea any of this had taken place. All he knew was that he was mad for being stood up when all he was trying to do was give the two men twenty-six thousand dollars for basically doing nothing.

What a bunch of divas, thought Steve. *My money isn't good enough for them?*

The men were now officially an hour late and Steve's patience was at an end. He started the car and made his way out of the parking lot.

Screw 'em, thought Steve. If they wanted to come after him, so be it, but he wouldn't make it easy for them. He'd put up a fight. In the past couple of days Steve might have been behaving less like a jerk, but he sure as hell hadn't forgotten how to stand up for himself.

Steve was about to enter the freeway when he noticed a young man standing on the side of the road. He held a sign that read FORMER LUMBERJACK. HUNGRY. ANY HELP APPRECIATED.

The young man had an eye patch, one arm in a sling, and was supporting himself with a cane. Christ, he'd been through the wringer.

Steve pulled over and rolled down his window.

"Hey, you're a lumberjack?" said Steve.

"Yeah," said the young man.

"Me, too," said Steve.

The young man's face lit up. "It's a pleasure to meet you. I'm Jeff."

"Steve."

"Hey, would you happen to know if there's a secret lumberjack society nearby? I've been asking for days and no one around here seems to know anything. I really need a job."

Steve smiled. "You're looking at it," he said. "Get in."

The young man dropped his sign and hobbled over to Steve's car. Steve reached across the passenger seat to open the door for him.

As he gingerly lowered himself into the car, the young man let out a small yelp. Man, he was busted up good.

"I'm so glad I found you," said the young man. "Thanks for stopping."

"No problem at all," said Steve. "Always happy to help out a fellow lumberjack. You like pizza?"

Steve handed the young man one of the pizzas and the young man grabbed a slice.

"So what do we do now?" he said.

"Now," said Steve, "we have a tree to chop down. After that, I'm not sure."

"Sounds good," said the young man.

Yes, Steve thought. *That does sound good.*

60

It was business as usual at the pool. Tyler was rubbing sunscreen on his face and people were swimming. Chester walked in wearing his swim trunks and several gym members applauded. They sure did love that Chester was now swimming on a regular basis.

Tyler had always admired Chester, even before Chester started swimming again. But Chester had recently inspired Tyler, too. Tyler realized that if Chester could start swimming again, then maybe Tyler could stop urinating in the pool.

And Tyler was on quite a roll with it, too. What had it been? Ten days since he'd last relieved himself in the pool? It's not like he'd ever really enjoyed peeing in the pool or done it intentionally, it was just something he did, and he'd never felt the need to stop.

But after seeing Chester change, Tyler thought maybe he could also change. And he *had* changed! Ten days was nothing to sneeze at. And he had to admit, it felt good not urinating in the pool anymore.

It had given Tyler a jolt when he first learned the two men he'd met in Chester's office had been gunned down under mysterious circumstances. It had given the whole town a jolt. That kind of stuff just didn't normally happen where they lived.

But Tyler didn't want to think about that anymore. He wanted to think about all the fun everyone was currently having in the pool. He jumped down from his lifeguard chair and started walking the perimeter of the pool. He liked to make a few rounds every shift to stretch his legs.

His eyes landed on Harold and his parents. Harold was playing with two wooden boats.

"Mighty nice boats you have there," Tyler said to Harold.

"Thank you," said Harold.

"Did you get them for your birthday? I know you had a party not too long ago."

Harold's mother chimed in. "We actually found them in the lake by our house. They seemed to have been abandoned, so we decided to take them in!"

Tyler wasn't usually drawn to wooden boats, but the detail on these particular boats was downright impressive. One of the boats was blue and one was purple. One had the name STEVE painted on it, and the other had KELLY painted on it.

Tyler thought to himself that he'd never had toys that nice when he was a kid.

He'd never had anything that even came close.

ACKNOWLEDGEMENTS

Heartfelt thanks to
Almie Rose, Beccah Risdall,
Rob Getzschman, Cliff Weber, Pin

Made in the USA
Las Vegas, NV
04 February 2024

85308185R00142